And We

Never

Arrive

And We Never Arrive

By
Robin Nixon

Quill and Spoon Publishing

Published in 2013 by Quill and Spoon Publishing,

an imprint of CreateSpace.

ISBN 9780615886602

For Will

"The mind must not be divided into 'I' and 'this experience.'"

Wisdom of Insecurity
Alan B. Watts
1968

Prologue

"I want to come with you to the airport," Georgia announced over the phone.

"OK. But I am planning to leave in about an hour."

"I know. I'll get a taxi and bring it to pick you up."

"OK." *Is she crying?* Masterson's own voice was smooth and contained, but his insides were a yolk in mid-scramble.

He drifted downstairs to the deli on the first floor. Dusk was blending the storefront into the rest of the New York City street. His goal was a cup of coffee, maybe a candy bar, but plastic buckets of flowers were commanding the front stoop.

Which one? He fondled stem after wet stem, until the shop tender squirmed. And then returned to the flower he saw first. A yellow bud with pink on the tip. An everyday rose.

"Just one?" The owner looked him over.

Mac hesitated, and then nodded.

Up the stairs, lacking coffee, the question echoed around his head, taunting him. *"Just one?" Yes but...*

On the table near the phone, Post-Its sat, decidedly unpacked but beckoning him now. He peeled off a piece and carefully folded a non-sticky strip about one centimeter wide. He tore it off, creating a slightly uneven edge but not too bad, all in all. He fished a pen out of his carry-on and wrote in all caps.

Then, with fingers that seemed far too big and clumsy, he slipped the strip of paper deep within the bud's inside petals. She wouldn't see it until it blossomed fully. Until he had already arrived at his new home. In truth, he knew it should have been said long ago. But he also, rightly, knew he would lose courage at the airport. Addressing the flower, he asked aloud, "How long will it take you to tell her I love her?"

Chapter One

Bombay blue in plastic and Schweppes yellow in tin, he was clinging to the tropics for as long as possible. But the recycled air, dry despite its hand-me-down status, was equally intent on prying him away from the equator's proximity.

I remembered the presents, didn't I? Did I get everyone? Jeesus, I don't even know who is going to be there.

The magazine against the seat back stuck up above the tray table. The cover's flat ornaments gave a tin man whine: "If you only had a heart." Mac shoved it down, hard, deep into the pocket, but it refused to disappear.

But what can I bring them that they can't get here? Bringing gifts back in the other direction is so much easier. How sick everyone must be of getting gifts from Cambodia. How many silk scarves and Angkor trinkets can one family handle?

His entertainment panel flashed the exchange of confection for affection with Pavlovian delight. *And the other stuff, a couple of bottles of rice liquor and some jade to fill in for whomever I've forgotten. That stuff will be good for Cate and company, I think. But isn't it what I gave Mom and Dad last year? Do I look lazy? Will it look like I don't care? Am I lazy? Of course I care.*

He drained his cup and watched the butt of a flight attendant. It sallied and stopped. Turning off a call button, she stooped over a chair, giving Mac an excellent view. Suddenly, it swiveled out of sight as she started back up the aisle. Caught, his stare jumped to her face. *Look at those striped cheeks. What, is she going into battle or something? Defending whom, the tribe of cheer?*

Her uniform brushed against his elbow, calling his attention to his skin, an unfortunate reminder. At this stage in the long-haul flight, he had become clammy with a day's worth of oil production meeting a potpourri of tonics and lotions from the toilet room. After cursing himself for forgetting to pack his deodorant in his carry-on, he had resorted to putting "rainfresh toilet spray" under his armpits and melonberry lotion on his neck and arms. The overall effect, he concluded as the flight attendant swished away, was that he smelled like a rancid Barbie doll. *My poor neighbor, but to hell with it. She is asleep anyway.*

He glanced at her snore against the sunlight, a rebellion against the proper way to battle jet lag. *Or maybe she has been knocked unconscious by my stench. Being knocked unconscious doesn't seem that bad really.*

He closed his eyes. *Well, Dad seemed to really like the rice liquor last Christmas, so maybe I should "refresh" his supply. Will Mom think I am being insensitive to "his condition" by bringing him liquor? How bad is he anyway? Installing grab bars in the bathroom…it doesn't sound good. But isn't that an argument to give the poor man something*

4

that he will really enjoy? I mean, he's old, it's a fact, let the poor guy enjoy himself; what's the point of all this careful preservation talk?

Is liquor particularly bad for stroke victims? I should know this…He must be pissed. I'd be pissed.

But then I'll have to give something else to Cate's husband. Why didn't I pick up some of that new Cambodian pop before I left? I wonder if I could find it here? Possible. Maybe in NYC.

Giving up trying to pretend sleep, Mac shifted in his chair, banging the tray table in the process. His cup shook and the ice cubes talked back at him.

How old are the kids again? A year older than last year. Sure, but how am I supposed to know what they're into now? It's not like they write me. Would I've responded to a strange uncle living in a far-off and sinister-sounding place? Some random family member I only saw once a year? No. A chore in awkwardness, if I ever heard of one. Almost as bad as being expected to figure out gifts for children you barely know.

Crumpling the paper napkin, *my sisters' e-mails sound more like they are trying to one-up me than relate to me. Not that I relate to them either.*

The nip bottle shoved the napkin ball to the bottom of the cup, muting the ice. *But, of course, they will all have something useful or sentimental for me, stuff that won't fit into my bag, but I will be obliged to take, all the more so because my own gifts will not be nearly as thoughtful or appropriate. Why do I do this every year?*

Piling his trash and tray into one hand, he fingered through the seat back again. *I swear, this holiday is like a parasite. With a year life cycle. Making me crave things that just a month ago I was fine without.*

Alcohol, perfume, jewelry, cigars, and chocolate beckoned from two dimensions. "Release us from these duty-free pages, oh potent one, and gratify yourself with the luxury of our full size. Oh, what we can do for you, to you, if you will only let us see your worth—"

The magazine settled on his lap. *Should I try to hit on this girl?* He looked down at the closeness of their knees. *The flight attendant is cuter. But this girl isn't bad.* Her loose pants failed to hide a trim thigh. *And it's a terrific opportunity. She won't be outright rude. She has to sit next to me for another six hours after all.*

She was sprawled diagonally in her seat and her neck was arched away from him. Her forehead twitched against her fingers.

I already know a lot about her. She likes the pretzels. She is a vegetarian and has no qualms about eating her meal long before mine arrives. I think she was eyeing my yogurt at brunch.

She shifted onto her shoulder, closing her legs.

And she gets up for the bathroom with this pomp and pride, like she has an important errand scheduled or something. One that will advance her status in the world. "Here I am, and my body has to urinate!" What is she, two years old? Maybe she has a urine fetish, and that is why she always wants a different drink, orange juice, soda water, tomato juice, do-you-have-grape-soda…Erratic, compared to my steady gin-and-tonic-little-ice-please.

What would Ria say? What did Ria say? Oh, how did she put it? These ESL speakers somehow stumble upon such elegance…

Even in casual everyday thoughts, Ria has always been accompanied by sound effects. Recalling the most recent scene with her, he watched her bangs, straight and thick, swing to chime at the end of her point like a cymbal. Her foot stamped, and her eyes narrowed to a searing pitch. His bed had sprawled out behind her, waiting for her to cue harmony, but she stood, defiantly, in front of her round suitcase, packed but not quite zippered…

6

She has always come with music, unbeknownst to her. Stretching two years back, a Friday-night bar provided a stage for that same black hair. As her laugh tuned and warmed among friends, her hair had sung across her back like an opening act. Mac, who had just stopped in for a solo drink, became suddenly aware of the sweaty creases at his wrist, grime dusted with exhaust from the motorcycle taxi. *Shoulda gone home and showered after work...*

A Cambodian band was covering American pop at a volume that pounded away any hint that a world might exist outside these walls. Girls circled, as if on a conveyor belt, like one of those sushi places, little quivering pieces of bare flesh, sorted individually in different colored tanks, beckoning defenselessly to be grabbed and mouthed by you and your chopsticks. These girls, Mac knew, were specifically there in hopes of gaining his, or some other Western man's, interest.

But the girl with music for hair seemed there for the music. Instead of hovering solo, she stood close to a young man and woman, sharing nods and smiles with them. They paid no attention to the conveyor belt of raw meat.

She was a bit taller than the other two, but still petite by American standards. She was wearing a tank top herself, tight fitting but with broader straps than the circling sushi. In between songs, she surveyed the room with a toss of her hair, allowing her neck to peek out from the curtain. She did it a second time, twisting a little more, making eye contact with Mac, *did her eyelashes just flutter*, as she set down her beer glass on the bar.

Her friend, the male, had moved between Mac and Ria, perhaps with a plan to order, once he and Ria paused their conversation. The female friend, in capped sleeves and trousers, made up the far end of the isosceles triangle. She was listening to the other two, watching them for

7

clues for when it might be cool to check out the band again. Ria, with an amused smile, kept her focus within the triangle, although she must have felt Mac's stare. She did, however, leave her hand behind on the bar, a Hansel and Gretel trail of manicured fingers for this strange man to follow up her arm, over her shoulder, and into the hot oven of her neck.

The three were slender, looking about eighteen. However, that could easily be late twenties in these parts. They spoke French, slowly but more or less exclusively.

But what do I know. There could be scatterings of Khmer or even Vietnamese in what they are saying. I wouldn't be able to tell. Especially in this noise.

But there, he heard the mouthy jhhs and oouuhs, which are his definition of French. She swallowed as she listened to her friend, and anger briefly gleamed across her forehead. But it was only an act. She knew she looked attractive. She knew she was being watched.

For Mac, that anger sparkled with sugar, with its suggestion that her friend was not a romantic interest. It tempted Mac through the unlocked gate. Beneath the discussion, she felt Mac's eyes bicker upon the path between her hand and collarbone. With some barely perceptible stage fright, she took the cue and started to caress the bar, in the puddle of her glass's sweat, as if drawing a map to the gingerbread.

Mac mentally willed the other two away, pleading, *don't you two want to get closer to the band or something?* Yelling it in silence, trying to subliminally brainwash this obstacle. *But she might go with them. Oh, what am I doing? Don't get mixed up in this. You can't handle this right now. Just go home. But it is only nine. I won't be able to sleep for a long time yet...*

All right, one more drink. Only one more. It will take an hour for any service around here anyway.

Her curtain swung again. And yes, they did want to get a better look at the band. But be careful what you wish for. The boy hopped up on the stool next to Mac. His perch was aided further by a painful crank from his collar, like a lid on a hinge, his body strutting out behind. That fresh-baked neck, wafting vanilla, was now almost completely blocked from his fantasies of nibbling by an oily chin that had never known a razor. The other girl stood awkwardly, watching, cheering a few seconds behind everyone else.

This dynamic is impossible. Probably for the best. Anyway.

"Yes, I'll have another gin. One. A single. Yes, with ice. And with tonic. Tonic water. Like this one here. Gin and tonic. Together. Yes, a gin and tonic. One." Sigh. *But be polite; what if she turns this way?* He turned toward her, finding her making a show of enjoying and applauding the band, smiling broadly into the lights. Her face reflected the words, as she shone her American coolness forth.

Oh god, that's just too cute. Such cheese. How uncool such enthusiasm would be in the US of A. pop music. At least Mister Cranked-Chin here has got grunge right.

Plaid dimmed with dirt, and jeans that swallowed his tiny ass like some giant whale. His gelled hair was incongruent with his effort at looking effortless, but he had almost nailed the entire look.

But hey, dude, wash off the beachboy grin during this rendition of Barbie-let's-go-party. Sure it makes one tingle to see all those breasts bouncing to the beat, but, man, in that outfit it has got to be head-banging or bust, and even during that, don't you dare crack a smile. What is wrong with you? I thought all you kids out here were impeccably versed in MTV. You've obviously missed a few lessons.

Her over-shirt, *they call it a cardigan, right*, slid off the stool onto the floor. *Did she do that on purpose? Should I tell her? I can't go screaming into their group. Should I fetch it for her? Walk through them*

9

to her side? I can always pretend I have to go to the bathroom afterward.

Beach Boy Grin cranked his chin higher, in determined un-acknowledgment of Mac's passing, but the lid had closed tight, when Mac turned and gathered the puddled cardigan off the floor, as if it was a trampled puppy. "I think maybe you dropped this."

Ria had smiled and rolled her shoulders. Her friend had rolled his eyes.

Some smear of words about the band passed, while her friends pretended not to be watching them. Mac and Ria managed, somehow, to move closer to one another.

"So how do you know these guys?"

"We have a class together; our teacher is from Paris," she had bragged.

"Oh, you go to school together. What ya studying?"

"English mostly. Would prefer to study art or fashion or something, but can't. Not in school, at least."

"Why not?"

Grunge boy had piped in, "We all study English."

All right, dude, I am aware you can understand what I am saying.

Capped-sleeves puffed up to explain. "The scholarship from *L'ecole* is for language study. French and English," she finished quickly and took a step back.

"Well OK, then." Mac laughed at the vacated hole.

Ria took over, but kept her eyes on the band. "Some of our parents knew French, so that comes easy, but our teacher says English is more practical."

"True."

Grunge boy asked, "Do you speak French?"

"*Oui, en peux,*" Mac lied.

10

"Great, we still prefer French."

"Oh yeah. Why?"

He answered in French, rapidly. The only word Mac caught was *philosophique*.

"Uh sorry, I still prefer English."

"OK, how long you been in Phnom Penh?"

The slight grammar flub, even amid the perfect pronunciation, had lent a supportive hand to Mac's teetering ego. "Three years."

"Wow," and then smirking, "learn any Khmer yet?"

Mac looked away and nodded. And then quickly changed the subject, in flawless English, mind you. "So, what are your names?"

"Chanroth" had come with a grin.

A transient "Ria" had been framed by a bold stare.

Mac was asked to move the empty can and nip for a tray of plastic containers, wrapped in either tin foil or plastic. A fruit cup. A swallow of water. One container, on a metal hot plate, held some green beans among some gravy among some mash that hid, with its gelatin mask, hid something called, simply: beef.

What the hell was that other girl's name? Chanroth and that damned grin. I got pretty good at Khmer in the field. And that second year can't count. Do I even care about improving now? Then, I was just "settling in," now, maybe, I am "settling out." It is just too easy to get by with English.

This girl next to me could have been Ria. Maybe I would have bought two tickets. Maybe if I had invited her...What a loop that would have thrown in the old homestead train ride of made-up traditions. Mom might have teared with joy. Who knows?

The mash had some yellow film in its corner, yes, even with the gravy. And this yellow film turned out to be the best part of the meal. He dipped plastic green beans in it, getting an unwanted coat of gravy as well. He was picky for the first few minutes and then scraped every beige crevice with the spoon, even getting every last dot of the powders labeled salt, pepper.

Who am I kidding? There is no way I would have done that, invited Ria to share in my holiday pain. Shattered each side's reflection of me. Causing seven years' bad luck, saying nothing of all the bloody cuts at the outset. It's not like she is Georgia or something.

His neighbor was wondering if it might be possible to get the attendant's attention for her. *Sure, I'll be your hero, since you ask.*

She explained to the woman she would like some more water, and a juice, grapefruit if you have it, cranberry if not, thanks a lot, and, after all the requests and the departure of the attendant, a silence took over that made the plastic ware hitting plastic far too obvious. Beat, beat, and then much too late, as if she had been hoping the silence would just get less loud, she offered, "I always get so dehydrated in these things."

"Yeah, I think they are trying to keep people from getting up to use the bathroom." *Stupid asshole, you are the only one who knows this girl has gotten up every hour since you left Tokyo. Think of something nice to say.*

She helped him, or defended herself, with "But it is really unhealthy."

So is being cooped up in a flying sardine can for seventeen hours, so is a gin-and-tonic for every one of her bathroom trips, "So is everything, it seems these days."

"Yeah, the media makes it very confusing." She obviously had plenty to say on the subject but the sentence ended with a halt, throwing up a stop sign for the conversation she surely wished she hadn't started. His fork scraped at gravy mush, while hers stabbed at a pale grape. At

12

the end of her chew, she played nice again. "So what were you doing in Tokyo?"

"Actually I am coming from Cambodia."

"Oh reaaally." The attention paid to her fork dropped away; it continued to move steadily to her mouth in neglect. "What were you doing there?"

"I work there." *Shall I do the lines? Impress her. Do I still remember how to do this? The cocktail-party peacock feathers.*

"Wow. Doing what?"

Ugh, too easy. "I work for an NGO that is trying to stop malnutrition in Cambodia. My specialty is Vitamin A." *Fanned wide, notice me and all my virility.*

"Wow, wish I could do something like that someday. It's got to be tough though." She paused to let her fork put some dripping cherries in her mouth. "Your family must miss you." She chewed.

Shrugging, staring at her cherries, he echoed, "What were you doing in Tokyo?"

"Visiting my father; his business is finding a new market there, and he's not gonna make it back for Christmas, so…"

Mac let her tone conduct his nods, wondering, *why am I craving eggnog and donuts with red and green sprinkles? Are advertisements being broadcast from the pores of the already brainwashed?*

The flight attendant, and cart, finally came with her extra water and juice.

"Can I get you something to drink, sir?"

"Yes, could I have a gin and eggnog; please." *Nice, totally deadpan. What will she do?*

"I am sorry, sir, we are out of eggnog. Can I suggest tonic, sir?"

"Oooo-kay, but I was trying to get into the spirit around here."

"We have a variety of spirits, sir, but no eggnog. Rum, cognac…"

Jeeesus. "What is this, still Asia?"

The surrounding seats gasped and he felt his luck with his neighbor evaporate. Mac sighed, straightened his back, and stolidly faced the chair in front of him. "Gin-and-tonic-please-little-ice."

Three loudly efficient moves and, "Here you are, sir. Happy holidays." *Nice, totally deadpan.*

Chapter Two

New York City. The euphemism for his "final destination." He was to have a night here, if the weather had cooperated. But delay, delay, and an overnight in Tokyo instead. It is already Christmas Day. He was supposed to be on the rooster-rising Chinatown bus this morning, having accounted for skewed sleep, jet lag, and a nostalgic night in a nearby hostel on Houston Street. But no, now he is racing to get home by dinnertime.

Why didn't I just buy a ticket for a connecting flight? What is this ridiculous obsession with having time in the city to get my head on straight?

He had wanted to collect some sanity before facing his family, to visit some objective place between his worlds. But no, the bigger forces of entropy had conspired against his plans and he found himself instead approaching the ticket counter at JFK.

"Any chance I can still buy—"

"Nope."

The scalp didn't even look up; it had found the meaning of pattern baldness in the keyboard, the ultimate code for unlocking the destinies of generations of his family's men.

"So what you are telling me is that I can't get anywhere from here."

"Not todaaay." It's was a song, Mac realized, a tune the attendant had had stuck in his head all day. *"Can't get nowhere, nowhere (!), todaaaay."*

Perhaps tears of no creativity would have incited a glance, or a photocopied Greyhound schedule, but Mac's only thought was *shit, the buses are gonna be flooded too.* "Of course they are," the song continued in his head, *"It's Christmas Day! Don't ja know?"*

Ugh. A bleary wander through hallways, flashing the same newsstand over and over. *There are even more home magazines than last year. You are getting sleepy, sleepy, I tell you. Follow the flashing images. Find the perfect lawn mower...Maybe Santa will leave it in your stocking this year with a big shiny bow. But first, maybe you should surprise Santa with a little something this year. Just make sure, never to settle when asking someone to spend the rest of her life with you. Not to mention a surprise will get you laid. And of course, someday, if you are good, that shiny lawn mower you've always wanted.*

All right, come on, luggage and taxi. Oh, and call your mom. I don't wanna. Call your mom.

No pay phones anywhere. *Mom always claimed she could read my mind anyway; why does she still need me to call her? Mom! I am gonna be late. Sorry, the plane was delayed.*

Leaning over a counter wrapped with magazines, a clerk explained that the nearest pay phone is in Terminal C. Being the fifth Terminal A newsstand coming from either direction, there were no

16

customers. Never any customers. Thus, it was Mac's luck that the clerk was bored enough to notice Mac's subtle jet-lag-induced swoon. "Hey, man. Why don't you use my cell phone?"

"Really?"

"Sure."

The phone's buttons might as well had been labeled in Khmer...He felt like a child poking at a strange object, until the clerk finally took over, dialed for him and handed the phone back over just as Mom was answering.

"Hello," she said a second time, now with panic instead of flirtatious cheer.

"Mom, it's Masterson...Merry Christmas to you too...No, I am not there yet...I'm sorry...It's not my fault. The plane got delayed in Tokyo...I am sorry...By six...I'm sorry...Bus...There aren't any flights. Mom, I gotta go, or I'll never get there...This nice man's cell phone...I am sure it is expensive; that's why I should go...I will...Yes, I will...No, it's just me. Mom, I really gotta go...Caramels? ...'K, I'll try...You too...Bye."

"It never gets any better, does it?" The clerk looked at his phone.

"That *is* better." *Woo-hoo, what do we have here, a fellow commiserater? I should be working on these damn holidays, behind a counter, where I can't hurt anybody...*"What do I owe you?"

"Nothing."

"Come on; she'll ask me. What do I owe you?"

"Lie."

"All right, thanks." He pushed off, to join the circus, but turned back, his brain still echoing the phone conversation, "Hey, do you sell caramels here?"

"Caramels?" he sneered, his nose and forehead tracing the question mark.

"Right; sorry. Thanks again."

"Wait, do you mean these?" He pointed to the bottom row of the counter, the gutter to all the home magazines. Little tan rolls, mummified, sardine-pressed next to one another, baring their insides, stuffed with white paste, and collectively, incestuously, wrapped in one strip of cellophane.

"Uhh, I don't think so."

"Man," he said, giving Mac the once-over, "if I were you, I'd just buy them."

Mac felt a shiver run up his spine. He heard his mother's voice, her superstition, maybe-you-were-delayed-for-a-reason, you-never-know, something-terrrrrrrible-might-have-happened, been in the wrong place at the wrong time if you hadn't…stopped to buy some caramels.

"Fine," he stretched his hand to flip through four packs.

There was Cambodian riel in his wallet. And yen. And two single US, just enough to stop at the café for lunch in Phnom Penh, where most of the city preferred US dollars over inflation-prone riel.

Twelve dollars' worth of caramels on a credit card. *God bless America.*

The plastic bag, announcing the Big Apple Newsstand(s), swung from his wrist as he stumbled through customs and upon baggage claim. The latter was a trapeze act without the high wire. Suitcases somersaulted out the shoot to bounce upon a circling net.

He had almost missed his flight, running late as usual, but, *heh,* that meant his luggage jumped out among the first. Mac shouldered the duffel bag and left all those responsible timely people, including the vegetarian pee-lover, in his dust.

Automated doors responded to his touch, but found nothing worth keeping. He abandoned the oversensitive rubber carpet for cement, and looked for luck at the taxi stand. At the head of the line, a revolving man played cupid, mating weary passengers with horny taxis. Swaying back and forth, Mac waited for his fate.

Here we all go again. Didn't we just do this? Right, about a year ago, wasn't it?

His luggage traded him a hat for the caramels, but otherwise Mac decided he was enjoying the bite of weather through his short-sleeved polo.

See, addressing everyone in line, especially the guilt-ringing Santa against the door, *see how much I don't belong here. I am not even dressed properly.*

But no one looked. The only thing answering back was the blizzard of carols coming from both the terminal's outdoor speakers and some kid's incessant snowman. Even brake lights taunted him with red cheer.

Am I the only one who can tastes ipecac in all this drippy syrup? Am I the only one tempted to purge in Santa's bucket?

But I wanna believe in Santa Claus. Really I do. I wanna believe there is someone out there, judging me, deciding my worth. I don't want to be responsible for that evaluation...

Chapter Three

The corners of hip-length jackets swung menacingly. Blindingly. There was a hand reaching down, but the glove made it all feel impersonal. Shop windows of wonder flashed between coats and swinging arms. Entrances hummed carols. Intermittent faces at his height, or thereabouts, passed by, also in tow.

Who has been better this year? Who does Santa like more, you or me?

Feet were everywhere, stomping through slush; the gripes of treads drowned out any overhead conversation. But a bell was getting through. *Where's the bell?* It had to be somewhere through this knot, this mess of dark felt, fur, fleece, buttons, belts and boots, dotted with the occasional flirtation of a holiday scarf or stocking cap. The lifeline out of anonymity was in his fingers, but that bell, he could see it now, was in a white glove, supported by a white fur cuff, and *yes, could it be*, a bright red sleeve. Yanking, *Dad must not have seen; there is Santa Claus, right there, in the flesh, the real thing, beard and all.*

He tugged at the leather sleeve. But Dad didn't seem impressed. *Are big boys not supposed to get excited about Santa? Is not getting excited about Santa even possible?*

"Dad!"

"Hold on to me, Masterson. Don't let go. You hear me."

"But Daad! It's Santaaah!"

"No, it isn't."

"Ya huh! I need to tell him about the Raleigh Chopper!"

"It's too late. Santa's already done his shopping. Come on. Hold on to my hand."

Huge buttons, a long one, hugged by yarn, scraped Mac's face as his father tried to move against the tide. He yanked Mac's arm, maybe too hard, but Mac followed. He knew he had to be a good boy, especially this close to Christmas, but Santa was *right* there!

"That's not Santa."

"Then who is it, Dad, huh, who is it?"

"An elf; come on, Mac, we are gonna miss our train."

Another little boy, a tad smaller than himself, put money in the red bucket. The bell-ringing Santa smiled at him. A promising smile.

"Dad, puhlllleeaase," yanking back on the arm, letting the fingers slip.

The man turned around to see wet eyes under sandy hair. Thick white cap and rosy cheeks, a Norman Rockwell sight, if he subtracted the running nose. He checked his wrist; if he had been alone there would be plenty of time, but Masterson always needs to be dragged. "Puhleease, Dad," and then in a flash of brilliance, "It's Christmas Eve; pleeaase."

It *was* Christmas Eve. "Aww right." There was another train after all, she'd understand, the girls wouldn't notice, the lasagna would keep, better than a blubbering boy for the next half hour.

Giving Mac a dollar, he stood at the outer edge with a few other proud parents, walling in their young Santa spectators against the rushing crowd. He could have just as easily been at the zoo.

Mac cautiously approached the tower of red and white, hope personified, how pure the beard is, he *must* be magic. Timidly staring, not losing a blink to the Santa-like elf, as he tripped the bill into the bucket. He couldn't get a word out, and had forgotten anyway all about the dragster bike in the volume of the bell. He backed away, still staring, hypnotized by the personification of a candy cane, endowed with every sweet privilege and a hooking connection to Santa Claus. *Pleeaasse tell him I was a good —*

Suddenly, there was a hard something in his back, a leg, a smelly leg, and a blanket where a coat should be. A flaccid face peered down from stubble and creased eyes. The pupils faded. The crust around the lips was made wet again.

With rancid breath, "You gotta dollar there for me too, boy? I need a coat more than Santa does, don't you think?"

Screaming until this stranger was replaced by his father. He was suddenly picked up, hushed, saved by the familiar leather shoulder. Mac sealed his eyes closed against his father's scruffy neck despite his head's bounce atop his ride's brisk walk. A block was crossed. Through tears, slush-filled gutters striped asphalt. In the station, he was put back on the ground.

"You're getting heavy. Stop crying."

Mac said nothing, sniffling, feeling unworthy of the tiny jingle bells resonating from the station's speakers. *Why did Santa let that happen?* The boy was silent through most of the half-hour train ride. The ventilation dried his tears to his cheeks and the snot to his glove.

"Who was that, Dad?"

"Just a man."

"But why was he like that? Why didn't he have a coat? Somebody take it?"

"He was a crazy person."

"Why's he crazy?"

"Probably born that way."

Relief. The reverberation from the man's towering impact slowed. Mac and the stranger switched sizes, until Mac towered above him, proudly deciding, like Santa Claus, if the man deserved a dollar...

Chapter Four

Remember being proud? What a trip.

Mac was mated with a taxi that smelled of curry, and that had snow crusting its seams. Playing cards dangled from the rearview mirror, one of Shiva and one of the Virgin Mary. The way they were dancing implied Mary might not be a virgin for long. Garland was strewn along the dashboard. Red and green of course, but sparkling gray in the sudden sunshine outside the terminal. The driver giggled festively over his cell phone, speaking Hindi so thick and loud, Mac blamed the conversation for the smell of curry.

Gotta get there before dinner, or what was the point of all this. Two days' worth of travel, and all the headaches at either end. The ticket was a budget disaster. Why did I wait so long to buy one? Tonight is gonna be a diet disaster. Hell, the whole week is gonna be. Cookies everywhere. Mom's pecan pie. Huge US portions.

Pizza. How can I work pizza in somewhere around the lasagna and roast beef? Don't want to insult anyone, but only got so many days, so many meals...I am gonna come back a stuffed pig. Ria will be glad she left me. Not that Atkins would be so proud to hear about the rice and sweetened-condensed milk I live on in Cambodia. Not to mention gin and tonic. Angkor Beer. Mmm, but pizza...

"Hey, excuse me. Sorry, don't mean to interrupt. But is it too late to go to Times Square instead of Chinatown?"

The taxi driver only removed his cell phone far enough from his head to make a circular sway, a nod, a shake, and everything in between. "Wherever you want to go, is OK by me." The meter was running after all.

Two blocks from Port Authority, a glass counter revealed two pizzas, each a little aged but looking like heaven. There was a fresh tomato one with cloud-white slabs of mozzarella and a shiny spinach pie haloed by a spiral of mushrooms.

"What? No pepperoni?"

The place looked like it hadn't seen a customer yet today and wasn't expecting one. All the dirt was from yesterday, and the TV was turned up loud. The pizza man was wearing his apron-like pajamas.

"Naah." *It's Christmas Day, don't ja know?*

A slice of each pie went sliding, from a large wooden spatula, into the oven, to reheat until bubbly, out again, onto overlapping paper plates and wax paper, all topping a red tray, complete with napkin and a "want-anything-to-drink," without the man missing a single flash from the television screen. *We are not in Kansas anymore, Toto.*

A balancing act to the table: *please no Diet Coke on my crust.* He found a shaker of dried red-pepper on top of the garbage can and settled into a booth behind the garbage, facing away from the door, away from the man and TV, parallel the slimy mirror. The two slices could not get

25

enough pepper. He covered them red, shaking, pounding the container; *would the guy notice if I just took the cover off and dumped the flakes directly?* And the huge slices, warm, chewy, filled his stomach with a tasteless thud. Even the Coke had no flavor. He has to stuff himself to get any sensation out of eating anymore.

He tried not to think of Georgia, the Georgia of seven years past, giggling drunk, as she stretched the cheese from a slice, with her fingers, to see how far it would go. Could she make it vibrate? Could they make a pizza instrument, did he think? Dangling from a piece of pepperoni, that cheese continued to stretch, they were both in disbelief; it had to be the cheesiest piece of pizza that ever did exist; they should call the Guinness Book of World Records; did those people work at 3:00 a.m.? They should if they took their job seriously, now, shouldn't they. And oh my, she put the slice of meat between her lips, plucking the string of cheese, until her tongue became jealous. Mac watched the pepperoni disappear, along with a swirl of mozzarella, to a place he had yet to go. He had never wished to be processed meat so badly in his life.

Whatever. Her loss. Greasy plates, wax paper, crumbs, and flakes, were forced through the swinging flap of the garbage can.

It was suddenly cold out. The sky had become ruffled with wind, and the duffel bag caused him to coat with sweat. *How do these people put up with this weather? How did I ever put up with it? Two blocks 'til Port Authority. Two long blocks. Sixth and Seventh Avenues. There's a way to do this underground, isn't there? What, and miss all the Christmas decorations?*

He pulled his hat down over his ears. He could still smell the curry taxi in its wool.

Chapter Five

Logan Airport. A nineteen-year-old Masterson Peters stood in line at customs, with a backpack lagging down as if it was trying to hump him doggy-style. Passing weight from one foot to the other, his balance wobbled. The lines were moving so fast. And there was already so much to buy, so many magazines, so many choices of candy bars. Colors, ads everywhere, brightly flashing wants, even from across chests and shoes. Polished uniforms and sparkling clean hallways. Sterile counters and covered drinks. *Everyone is so fat.*

He was excited to be home, and simultaneously felt a superiority over all his compatriots who, he supposed, had never seen what he had seen. With wise pity, he watched them. Their fatigue dripped over mobile IVs of caffeine and sugar. Gadgets were wielded and scarves studied like poetry, as bookshelves were searched for portals into success. The shoppers had no idea how much they had. And they looked hungrily for more.

But not Masterson. He hadn't even needed to check luggage. All he owned had fit in the overhead compartment. One deflated backpack. And it was mostly presents for his family. Not to mention the huge package of pictures he had developed in Nepal. Other than that, just a few T-shirts, a sweater, half a dozen boxers, three pairs of socks, and a change of pants. Some standard toiletries, all proudly replaced, *I can actually live this way,* in Katmandu. A camera. He had even given away his Lonely Planet before leaving.

Four months ago, a lifetime ago, he had left this airport with so much more than this. It had seemed like nothing at the time. Leaving for four months with only one bag. Bursting at the seams. And one carry-on, of course, full of entertainment and education for the plane ride, during which he had slept, ate, and stared out the window. But, in the belly of the plane, his framed backpack, carefully chosen to have the most hooks and straps, had rocked like a stone of indigestion. Because how does one leave for Nepal without an extra pair of hiking boots, several sweatshirts, flip-flops, a motley of reference books tracing the historical origins of Hindu and Buddhist mythology, philosophy, metaphysics? Heavy pants, light pants, dressy pants? First aid kit, sewing kit, survival guide? Medication to combat malaria, altitude sickness, motion sickness? Mosquito repellant, water purification tablets, standard antibiotics, a half pound of licorice jelly beans, an empty journal, envelopes, extra pens, a load of unlined drawing paper, eight novels of different genres, a Walkman, twelve specially arranged mixed tapes, study-abroad itineraries, and all the essentials the program had recommended packing? He had given away all but the last within the first month of prep work in India.

That first month. Crossing his first street in Delhi, a barefoot, pregnant woman, shoveling tar and pavement, had torn at his clothes and heavy bag. An arthritic man had begged for aspirin, and when refused, had switched to requests for Tylenol. Gypsy children had chased him relentlessly, some missing a hand, or a knee, doubling backward, using scrap metal as a cane. Faces, floating within *saris* and *ferreds*, had watched him from lives so different than his.

He had become lost in how much he didn't know. Could never know. His own eyes, his own knowledge, had disintegrated in the pollution to be batted around by honks and chatter. They had all stared back at him in a ravenous raucous of rickshaws and raja men, gobbling him up alive, digesting him and shitting him out in an indeterminable splatter, laying a film on the river of railroad tracks, and beading the sweat on the destitute scalp that had agreed to guide him back to his group. He had become lost in more ways than can ever be found.

What use am I? What can I give? He had wanted to open a vein, a full pulsing neglected vein, and let the starving suck at it, until he was depleted and they were full. Instead, he had slowly parceled out the weight of his bag in a series of presents along his way.

The clothes had been the easiest to pass on. T-shirts and pants found homes easily in the streets of Delhi. He had carried his sweatshirts 'til they were up in the mountains. A Nepali girl, asking for money, received one, when she explained how cold her mother got at night; she was a pretty and precocious nine-year-old, with probably more English than was in her best long-term interest, but for now, she had eyes that saw everything and knew how to strike a stake at a heart's pocket.

The English books had mostly gone to other travelers, some within his program. The heaviest ones had been given to a charity house, specializing in used books and targeting backpackers. Masterson hadn't been convinced it was an actual charity unless the three guys, who ran the storefront, were the recipients. Their shop consisted of shelves that folded in on one another if they decided to close shop. Most nights, however, all three slept on a mat on the sidewalk in front of the open shelves.

The Walkman, tapes, and drawing paper had gone to an adolescent at a monastery, and the jelly beans were unleashed into chaos among a pack of tiny beggars. A clinic had tried to compensate him for the medications, and a mother thanked him for the needles, thread, and scissors, but had handed back the first aid kit in confusion.

Feebly trying to unload the weight on his back, he had taken, in return, the knowledge of how much he could do without.

Upon arriving home, he was feeling painfully nostalgic and in love with his common man, forgiving their ignorance and discontent. He remembered being panged with wants before he left, and now he had returned with the knowledge that he had everything he could need. He was gaunt with his first parasite, but felt no craving, no slap of heart-attack rebuke at the sight of the icing-slobbering walnut-stuffed cinnamon monstrosity, an indulgence he had devoured minutes before his out-going flight, sort of a "last meal" before falling off into the unknown. Instead, he met it with curiosity; why would he want such a thing? Why would he spend time even thinking about it? Rice was enough. Maybe a little *dahl*. He felt in control of himself, at peace with his desires, clarity, a rising above the thrashing of daily longings, freed from the I-could-really-use-a-cup-of-coffee-when-is-Mom-gonna-get-here, to oh-so placidly reflecting on the state of humankind.

In all honesty, he felt a bit like Santa Claus; a bag full of gifts and a peacefully patronizing smile. Full with epiphany. *This is how I will be for the rest of my life. The birth of my true personality.*

He would be the intriguing uncle to his future nieces and nephews, and the guiding shoulder to his older sisters. His father would pinch his mother with pride over their only son, as he entertained them
30

all with exotic descriptions of yak meat, butter tea, ubiquitous fennel. Tales of adventure and serendipitous discovery. His mother, late night, over hot chocolate, would admire her son's sensitivity, as he explained his heartache for the suffering poor and his resolve to *do* something.

Hugs arrived in the airport, warm, fleshy, and perfumed. The faces seemed foreign with familiarity and spouted, "It is so good to have you back safe and sound…didn't you eat anything while you were gone…" A passenger-seat ride through straight lines of snow, glossy roads, orderly traffic lights, rules, and etiquette, so, so many brand-new cars, led to arrival back at the homestead, a place that seemed like a pin in the haystack he had just discovered. The house was warm and tight with memories. He was to hang a youngest child's ornament on the tree and pass out hugs all around. "Sooo, what was it like?"

He felt like the walls of a uterus with a baby that wanted to come out. *How does this all fit though here?* "Uhh, wanna see?"

He rummaged to the bag's bottom, reliving all the painstaking effort he took to have all these pictures developed and organized, so the moment he arrived, when the questions were still hanging in the air, he could show them all the beauty he found in the beggar's open hand, the Nepali girl's eyes of English dreams, the snake-charmer's chapped mouth, the baby's leg wrapping desperately around the swollen belly and hipbone of his slightly older brother…

"I don't know, Mac. I mean these pictures are kinda a downer." Cate didn't want her fiancé's first Christmas Eve with them spoiled. "Why don't we put them away for after the holidays?" Starving children and rotting lepers does not a festive holiday make. And besides, it was time for the holiday feast.

"So there's no happy people in India, huh." His eldest sister's husband, Slade, clapped him on the shoulder as they headed to the kitchen.

Cate related the difficulties of the real estate exam, and Mac felt sick to his stomach. What had he done? He was suddenly a stranger at the table that still held the scars and smudges of his childhood. A double-decade squiggle, etched from a toy battery-powered pen, still curled under the plate that was now boasting more food for his one person, than had been served for his entire host family. Half the plate was filled with a slap of roast beef, glistening with melted fat, and still a little-girl pink on the inside. Good-luck lima beans spilled upon the rest of the porcelain; their cheekiness chastised, in one corner, by a whip of potatoes. Against the rim, his mother was heaping his sister's asparagus casserole into a mountain proudly marking due north. A whole new plate was needed for the bread.

"Well, Mac, looks like you're just gonna have to wait for salad," his mother teased. More food than he had seen in one sitting in months. "We decided we would save lasagna for tomorrow night."

Cate noticed his wet eyes, "Don't cry; you are back now. No need to worry; no yak butter here."

They all laughed, and she had the floor again. "I mean, it is a year away still, but I want—"

In his sudden hatred of them, he couldn't help himself. He interrupted her professional update, with an announcement that he wouldn't be finishing his degree in mythology. He wanted to do something actually useful. Like medicine or something.

His oldest sister, a lawyer, nodded. "It's nice to feel like you *might* be helping someone, but it is hard to know if—"

His father put his hand on Mac's shoulder, "Finally becoming more practically minded, son; I'm proud of you. How long have I been

32

telling you there is no money in academia, not to mention jobs? Now, a doctor on the other hand, there's job security in that."

"You don't have the grades to be doctor," Cate quickly informed him. "Grades are important, ya know. Don't underestimate them. Like, if I get a high score on this real estate exam…I'll have a shot at working with the best of the best in our area and that would be such a great stepping-stone for me…'Cause what I would really like is to open up my own office someday."

"Now that would even give you the flexibility to start a family." His mother smiled flirtatiously at her second child's catch.

Giggles among the girls. Masterson slouched into his chair, forgoing the thin gravy, as the plans for the wedding were tiptoed through, with shrieks to be careful occurring around the meant-to-be surprises.

Chapter Six

The tunnels of the Port Authority bus station were buzzing, whizzing, with the same corridors repeating themselves. Peter Pan needed help getting everyone snuggled in tight but Tinkerbell and her fairy dust were nowhere to be found. The place was swarming with lost boys, and Mac, with his belly full of pizza, was among them, trying desperately to understand what Captain Cook did with his gate number. *The greyhound ate it,* the pirate snickered.

Orange numbers and yellow ones, and white ones, and a set of stairs, *going up or is it down, and is that the same ticket counter or another one?* The clocks were all off from one another, but there was a dragon-length of people looking confident, wrapping around a wall, *this looks familiar, right?* And sure enough, following the spiked line, there was "Boston express" written in orange, with several numbers, among them noon, and a 42. His exit had been found, but it seemed the whole crowd wanted to walk this particular plank. A litter of college kids were

34

busy ignoring one another. Wasted couples teetered here and there. Anonymous joes. And several Spanish babies. With their mothers in tow.

But the fork of the dragon's tail was sharp with a uniformed man who cornered Mac into a plastic booth. Mac was frisked with his metal detector, while his partner "relieved" him of his bag.

"Where you going, sir?"

"Boston. Like everyone else."

"What for?"

Uh, it's Christmas; don't ja know? But fatigue and airport habit took over. "Pleasure."

"Pleaah-sure." A smirk. "Where do you live?"

"What is this?"

"Nothing serious. Just a security measure. Some pranksters seen *Speed* too many times."

A bomb on a bus. A hurling threat halted by an immobile hero. "Shoot the hostage...Take her out of the equation." *So this bulbous man is Port Authority's version of Keanu?*

"This is some humbug's idea of a joke," the man continued, revealing that he had humanity all figured out. "This scrooge has been calling in these stories all week; he's just wants attention."

The guy's partner muttered at Mac's bag, "If you ask me, it's Santa giving us some overtime."

The interrogator ignored him, unswerving in his scrutiny of Mac. "Where you live?"

"Cambodia."

"Cambodia!" Eyebrows raised, voice heightened to get his comrade's attention. *Hasn't that place been wiped off the map?* "Long way to come for pleasure."

"You telling me?"

"What, the girls ain't pretty enough for you over there?"

"Why don't you go and find out?"

"Why you in New York City?"

"Why you in New York City?"

"Look it, man, this form needs an address. Can't put no Cambodia."

"How's Houston Street?"

"Fine."

The dragon's tail was slithering away, flipping and flopping in hungry anticipation.

Noticing his hook had lost Mac's attention, the guard patronized, "Don't worry; there's no way all them people are getting on that first bus." And then prodding his captive further, "So what you doing in that war place anyway? I thought thems people hate all white people there."

"There's no war there anymore."

"You sure."

"Huh?" Turning his face from the tail, "Yeah, I'm sure. I'm the one who lives there, remember."

"Or at least you says you do. Your name?"

"Masterson. Peters."

"Why you got two last names? Your mom sleep around?"

Mac looked him over. Rent-a-cop. With a gold chain. *What they paying you to work on Christmas?* His paunch revealed insecurity as did the ring of purple at his eyes. Briefly, Mac imagined him in profile, lit by the yellow-green light of late night infomercials and saturated with beer and potato chips. But right now his sallow skin was being pushed around his cheekbones, with the pleasure of authority, ready for a swordfight.

All right, I dare you, go ahead, keep me from going home. "Mom, I was arrested..." Now that would throw a kink or two into the "traditions." "Should we wait on dessert for you honey, you have to tell me now, because I want the pecan pie to be warm; we don't mind

36

waiting, but keep in mind your father needs to go to bed early, and so do the kids, so when exactly will they let you out of jail..."

"Hey, can I go now?" The flames of the door were open and Peter Pan beckoned the rest of the dragon aboard with a sinister smile.

His sidekick looked up from messing through the bag, and they exchanged looks. If they kept him, they would have to skip lunch, and get the real cops. "He's clean."

"Yeah, you can go. Go get yourself some pleaaasure." A disgusting snort, thick and heavy enough to stick to Mac's stuff.

He shouldered the bag without zippering it and chased the flirtatious whip of the suddenly taut tail.

Wish I was running after pleasure. Running away from possible hell, is more like it.

He gave the bag's zipper a tug, getting a fleeting moment of accomplishment when it went all the way up in one swoop, and in almost one continuous motion, he swung it over to the man pushing at the Greyhound's belly. "Thanks," and up the stairs.

All the seats looked busy. But there was a maltreated one about three-quarters back. An aisle seat with a bag in it, but the ma'am doesn't have a choice. There was etiquette after all.

"Excuse me." *Prepare to deal with my existence.*

"Oh, I am sorry," the woman said, feigning stupidity, and moving the reindeer's home to her lap. Its bow hat wobbled atop plush antlers. Martyrdom.

Mac sat and felt the pizza, melted mozzarella not ingested since the last time he was in the States, blow bubbles into his intestine. Maybe he won't end up being as anonymous on this bus as he hoped. But the dirty aisle, railed by fake leather coats, a ball of yarn, rustling Doritos bags, a supersized milkshake, baby caps, a horned bracelet, a toddler's kicking feet, a skull-stickered tape deck, a frayed knee, sweat socks, an eight-year-old's tongue, and a gigantic spilling thigh, reassured him that, most likely, for the next five hours he will be no more than "some guy."

Chapter Seven

"A master's of science now?" The lines in the professor's face were heavy, as if the holidays had only fattened the creases. He sat at his desk in short shirt-sleeves; yellow-crusted pores lined his eyes. "But the stories you were tracing in Nepal had promise."

"*To whom?*" Mac wanted to retaliate, but how do you ask such a thing about someone's life focus? "Yes, it seems that Ramayana can be found even in the smallest temples, although in some places, especially in the mountains, it gets mixed with pagan sacrifice. It all gets very blurry, ya know? Like, everyone just believes in it all, like they are covering all their bases or something."

"Of course. But it's not what they believe is true that is important, Masterson. It is how the story has been changed."

"But if you tell them a different way of telling the story, they just say that one is good too. How can a change mean anything if it is all good, was just as good before, as it is now—"

"But a change implies something; things don't just change for no reason. After all, 'once in motion…'" he waved at the theme lifted from physics. "They already know what the tale means to them; they don't have to articulate it to you. It is *your* job to figure out why a certain version is preferred, not theirs. And the only entrance you have is to start by looking at the deviations."

"But what if it's just a 'telephone effect'?" Academia's ready reliance on the experiments of schoolchildren: a secret whispered through a chain of ears can be radically, and randomly, different when it comes out the other side. "Sometimes I think even genes go through the telephone effect. I think Darwin would agree."

"Genes?" His mythology professor stared at him for a moment and then sighed. "Yes, that is where the focus is nowadays. Mechanism. How come it is this way or that way? It's all about 'why'; what about 'should'?"

"'Should?'"

"Do you understand me? We need people who care about the big questions, the questions of justice, the need to continually define right and wrong, about the history of how it has been defined; how it should be defined today."

"I care, it's just that…"

"All right, if you care so much," the professor spit out fast, before checking his agitation. He paused and then continued in his classroom tone, "Is Rama behaving admirably or not?"

"Uhhh…it depends."

"On what?"

"On which part of his story. On who you ask."

"I am asking you. Is Rama acting admirably? Is he a good judge of right and wrong? Would you follow him?"

"I can't judge Rama. He is from a different time period, a different culture. Perhaps I would have done what he did in his circumstances, with his perspective. It's fiction, after all; who's to say definitively what is right and wrong?"

"It's-more-than-fiction; it-is-a-myth," the professor grumbled, repeating his own lecture notes.

"Still. It provides no concrete answers."

"So why bother with it, right? If it's not 'definitive,' no one is interested…Nowadays, people aren't looking past what's the right thing to have for lunch." The professor looked at his desk and found himself steadied by its boredom. "Come to think of it, I can't blame you for wanting to go into nutrition. At least people will find you interesting."

A long pause followed.

Mac knew he was supposed to say something, but what? His professor searched his eyes, accusing him of selling out, having no backbone, and then the light in his own pupils wilted, losing all their energy to Mac's vacuum of fright.

"Do you know, Masterson, what my youngest granddaughter said over Christmas?"

"What?" he answered with relief, grateful to be freed to look down into his lap, to watch his own youth, his own innocence, drain into his sneakers.

"She said, 'Grandpa, why do you still study stories; haven't you read them all already?'" his voice quaked. "Previously I would have said, 'Of course, honey, but every time I read one, it is new again.' But this time I got stuck on the why. Why do I study stories when no one looks to them for guidance anymore, or even for explanation of the values of the past? Imagination is discredited; nothing has use unless it's 'concrete.' There is nothing but this vain fruitless desire for uninterpretable fact…"

His voice faded into a mumble, and Mac looked up. "I am sorry, but this just seems more pressing."

"Look, Masterson, you will drown if you follow in my footsteps today. I don't want that to be on my shoulders." He took a big breath, his chest rising, and his face becoming not quite callous, but the expressions took on an air of efficiency. "What do you need me to do? Have you fulfilled your entry requirements?"

"Well I was premed, briefly, in undergraduate, but I have never taken statistics…"

"Oh, what's a bunch of equations anyway? I am sure you can squeeze it in later. I'll talk to Dean Steinberg. Don't worry about it."

"Thank you." They made clear eye contact.

And then a hand flagged through the line of sight, "Don't mention it."

His mentor started brushing at the dust on his desk, and Mac slowly understood he had been dismissed. He was already down the hall when he heard, "Masterson!"

He hustled back, feeling squat with the weight of gratitude and regret, "Yes, Professor—"

"There's a condition."

"Anything," blubbering, "and I want you to know how much I've gotten out of being with—"

"Come back and let me know when you find out what I should be having for lunch."

Chapter Eight

Mac sat, wishing for Tinkerbell to dust his eyelids, as the highway dropped away behind him. But even cradled by Peter Pan, his head just rolled from one side to the other, his ears boxed by a hard cushion in a disposable liner.

Agitated, he pulled some work, academic updates on nutrition in the developing world, out of the small backpack he used as a carry-on, a bag so loyal and functional, its existence was taken for granted. If it happened to go missing for a second, however, Mac's pulse would halt.

The first report solemnly announced, "The bioavailability of vitamin A in fruits and vegetables is lower than previously assumed, especially if not consumed with fat or animal products." *Great, so our push to help families plant diverse subsistence crops is incomplete at best. How's that for a Christmas present?*

Off to the right, a small TV created a tunnel of vision with all the other TVs rowed near the windows. Against his will, he began staring at the tunnel's shadows, something about a dog and a grumpy cop, and guess what, yes, the dog helped the cop, and the humbug's heart grew threefold...

Mac felt like he had cotton candy on his eyes when the bus slowed, and the loudspeaker came on. They were all threatened with being left at the barn house of a rest stop for the remainder of their gawd-fearing lives if they were not back on this bus in fifteen minutes. No, she would not go looking for any of them, and she was not waiting for someone else to go find them either. She trusted they all knew how to read clocks. She had 2:45...

Bodies unfolded, and kids asked what was going on; is this Boston? One seat kitty-corner ahead, a Latina mother, sat very stiff, clutching a sleeping baby on-lap, like she had never had to pee at a worse time in her life and was praying to her grandmother, *please ask Jesus to get me through the next two-and-a-half hours*. Maybe he should offer to hold her baby later, watch her six bags and Pringles, so she could maneuver to the rocking metal harness they call a toilet-on-board.

But you forget, white man, you can't be trusted. Whatever. I gotta shit so bad I might be stranded at Ol' Nelly's Homestead for the rest of my god-fearing life. "Gawd-fearing," shit, I am broad-assed Bus-Madam-fearing. But maybe Old Nelly will inspire a conversion and I'll spend Christmas among the manufactured jams and lucky horseshoes.

Half the bus paid immediate homage among the aisles of French fries. The three o'clock call to fast food. A wheelbarrow was static with scented candles and, sure enough, plaid-covered jams. A row of pay phones stood at attention, marshaling in the line at the women's bathroom. Embedded between the sentries, a clown scale offered fortunes, but no one was brave enough to bear his cackle.

The omnipresent newsstand was on his left. Behind the counter, behind the rows of shiny candy bars, were more smokes than one could

44

imagine. A turnstile of sinister-looking lighters played Christmas carols on the countertop. And minuscule bottles of Jack Daniels sat mischievously in abundant packaging.

Naah can't be; they wouldn't be allowed to sell such a thing in a rest stop, would they?

But even when he returned from his shit, there they were: three nips of Jack in a package, flanked by a total of six caramel apples—*are they real?*—each wrapped again in its own right, three with nuts and three without. And hiding in the back was a mix for homemade ice cream, propped against red and green. *It's Christmas, don't ja know?*

In the frame of the clear front, there was a cutout of a nuclear family. Junior, dribbling into his ice cream, looked up into the smiling hovering face of Mom. She, in turn, handled an apple by the stick, behind her ass, as if hiding it from Junior. Meanwhile, Dad completed the triangle, smirking face-to-face with the whiskey. They were all dressed festively, creating a Christmas tree effect, with Jack the star. Or angel. You take your pick. Mac couldn't believe his luck and bought one. Just one. Thirty-five dollars. MasterCard was fine, of course.

A few drinks and maybe I will even get some sleep. Maybe even pull off some holiday cheer. Is this how people are doing it? Everyone's drunk? Except me. No wonder I'm so pissy.

With a new plastic bag swinging from his wrist, he almost gave Bus-Madam a cheery smile as he boarded. But then he remembered her first warning, involving intoxication and having "your arse meet pavement before you meet sober-ness." He figured he'd be getting in the spirit, in the metal can in the back, which had, after all, been provided by Peter Pan explicitly for his convenience.

In his seat, he buried his hand in the plastic. Picking through the packaging tape proved a challenge. The rustling bag seemed like it was echoing all over the bus, and, *what is this, a school-marm hard-on? Think about candy apples. No that doesn't work; cold ice-cream?*

The top of the box released suddenly, and the woman with the reindeer looked at him, annoyed at his elbow's jerk. Or was that suspicion? Excitement surged below, as he fondled through the bag. Under their cellophane, the apples were a little soft. He fingered their curves as he passed under their weight, and brushed against the wooden sticks to grasp a small plastic neck. He seduced it into his palm, engulfing the entire label, deflowering it from all its packaging, and forced it, hard, into the slit of his pocket. Then his left hand gave it a shot; it had more of a chance to get caught by probing eyes but also a little more elbowroom within which to maneuver. The contents were now loose inside the box, engorged; the fondling was easier, more relaxed. He found the spot he was looking for, aggressively wrapped a finger around it, and removed himself again. He thrust the second nip victoriously into his left pocket. *Save the last one for later.*

People stared incredulously as he stood up, with hands folded in front of his crotch, just as the bus was pulling out of the parking lot. Hadn't he just had a chance to piss at the rest stop? Got a problem down *there*, Mister? Or maybe they were just wondering if there was gonna be another movie, looking down the aisle to check on Bus-Madam's swollen ankle and thigh...

She saw him stand, and stepped on the gas to punish his stupidity. Teetering between seats, his hands abandoned their post and tried not to grip people's foreheads for support as she peeled out onto the highway.

There's no turning back now. He caught a sneer from the couple using the backseat, as he fell through the toilet-room door and closed it against them. In the green light, silver smudged at him from every angle. Several handles were bolted here and there for his safety. But he needed
46

both hands. With legs spread, swaying a little, facing a green version of himself in a smear of mirror, Mac unscrewed a bottle, and tipped the contents into his mouth. Nothing. He sucked a little and got a sweet lick from the rim. Crashing into the wall as the bus sped, he shook the bottle and persisted with his suck in spite of himself.

A worm of goo coated his teeth...He sputtered from betrayal. An attack on the bottle, but there, on its coat of arms, was its own defense. It read: Jerk Daniel's. And then, just for laughs, where Tennessee Whiskey should have been, it revealed, in a mimicking font, Caramel Topping.

Mirrored in vandalisms, Mac, coughing, vainly tried to crush plastic in his fist. He had more success in biting the rim off, but a slice retaliated into his lip. And a siren's balm of sweet declared his violence inappropriate. Spitting, he pushed the remainder of the bottle though a metal flap to meet used disinfectant wipes and sanitary napkins.

Can't believe I just paid thirty-five dollars for caramel topping; what did I do to deserve this?

Stumbling out of the bathroom door, he clutched the top of a seat. He ran his tongue over his teeth, grimacing, and furtively wiped his palm on a seat back. *I've lost my sweet tooth for this nostalgia nonsense; it's just all so freakin' sticky.*

Chapter Nine

The code breakers must be aware that everything important can be put in three or four words.

On the bus home from college, Masterson's mouth wouldn't stop smiling as it savored the first semester in the master's program. The nutrition basics were coming easily enough, aided by the plethora of good-looking girls, "eye-vitamins," in his classes. Statistics was dry and full of little freshmen he'd like to slug, but at least it made for good jokes...

The bus pulled into the beckoning lines of a parking spot. While waiting for the other passengers to gather their belongings and take their turns inching down the aisle, he could see his mother through the window. She was rocking back and forth, waiting to throw her arms around him and tell him about the Christmas decorations. She looked cute, in a red sweater, and a red coat, which was undone and flying around her. After greeting him, she complained of being hot.

48

"Well, take that coat off, Mom."

"But it's December!"

He laughed, and hugged her again. Even picked her up off the ground a little. He had a secret glowing in his heart and was waiting for the right moment to share its flame.

"Aah! Let me down," she said with a giggle.

The ride was smooth and the house was warm with the meal already started. Cate bounded downstairs, freshly showered.

"Thanks, Mom. The shower in the hotel was disgusting."

"You two could have just stayed here; there is plenty of room."

But the guilt slid right off Cate's shiny face. "We know, Mom. Maybe another time. We just wanted to—"

"They just wanted to have sex, Mom; nothing personal, you know." Mac interjected, always the diplomat.

His mother chuckled at the potatoes she was peeling, mocking the newlyweds.

"When the sex peters out, they'll be here all the time," he added.

He got a hard palm in the shoulder blade for that one.

"Hello, all," his oldest sister announced her presence, having let herself in and appearing suddenly in the kitchen doorway. "Man, it is cold out." The coat around her shoulders looked as if it might as well be on a hanger for all the body it was meant to protect.

"Where's your hubby?" Cate asked, bouncing a little, popping a grape into her mouth.

"He-isn't-feeling-well." The words came out as fast and as projected as the "hello all."

"What? And you left him all alone?"

"He's not that sick; he told me to come. He wants to be alone."

"No one wants to be alone on Christmas."

"How do you know? Are you everyone?"

"Now, girls," tried their mother.

Their baby brother noticed the fatigue in Inise's eyes clashing with the dreams of her younger sister, and chose sides. "Didn't you know, Inise; Cate *is* everyone. We are all just pawns on her chessboard."

Two female glares flanked Inise's guffaw.

"You try getting married sometime, and tell me it isn't a stressful experience; you try organizing all those people and let's see how Zen you stay."

"I'm not Zen."

"You just wish you were."

"No, I don't; I've never wanted to be Zen." But he was too happy tonight to continue this. "Besides, 'if you wish you are Zen, you are not Zen,'" he parodied.

"Well this Zen master is ready to become one with the food," Dad, entering from the other doorway, announced himself with a raise of his Tanqueray on the rocks.

"As long as you don't become *everyone* with the food." Mac poked Cate.

Cate ran out to get her husband, who had, once again, taken out the trash as an excuse to get a smoke. Mom was pretending to be appreciative, but usually she waited until the bags were full to their utmost capacity. The last two bags had been half empty. An obvious waste of plastic and how would it look, how would she look, when they didn't have enough bags to get through Christmas day with all that wrapping paper and another big dinner? But better to worry about garbage than worry about the smoke she smelled every time that boy Greg came back into her house…

After dinner, Mac wanted his mother alone. He offered to do the dishes and clean off the table, knowing his mother would help him. But
50

Inise counteroffered, insisting that she could see the honeymoon pictures later.

"Besides, it's kinda like I've already seen Barbados." She was talking into her wine glass. "We stayed in the Paradise suites in Las Vegas on our wedding night. We saved the Sphinx, the Pyramids, and the Venetian Canals for the next day's honeymoon."

"You hear that, honey, you could have seen three countries instead of one." Dad washed the wine around in his mouth, relishing the bargain price of his first child's wedding.

"Well, I can't wait to see the pictures," his mother announced, relinquishing the dishes to Inise, and settling in the living room to hover over the photo album. Cellophane-wrapped pictures were flipped through; ooo-ing accompanied Cate's verbal captions.

Mac knew he would have another chance. It was Christmas Eve, and on Christmas Eve, it was Mac's job to taste the desserts. Like every year, he must sally forth and explore the unknown in protection of the rest of the family, making sure the desserts were edible and not poisonous. And sure enough, when Inise joined them in the living room, Mac's mother called him into the kitchen with her.

Wiping suds off the counter, his mother mumbled to herself, "How did she use this much soap? Why is it every—" But upon seeing Mac, she slipped into her lines. "Are you ready; feeling brave this evening; there might be some pretty serious poison in these sweets, do you think you can withstand it?"

A jaunty "Ready-Mom," as he saddled up on a stool.

"There aren't any macaroons and—"

"I think I'll manage. Any pies?" He knows there are.

"Yes! Two!"

"Any ice cream?"

"Yes, but I need a brave explorer to tell me which one goes with what."

"But first you need to know if they are poison or not, right?"

"Of course."

She got out two pints, a butter pecan, and a french vanilla. Her knuckles looked like they might turn blue as she tried to get a grip on the frosty lids.

"Let the brave explorer do that," he offered, just as she had hoped.

"There is a pecan pie and an apple pie." She was bent over a drawer, looking for his baby spoon with the candy-cane handle.

"I met a girl, Mom." He licked french vanilla off his fingers.

"Oh really; that's nice." She handed him the spoon and turned her attention to the pies. Feigning disinterest, she hoped, would get her juicier details.

"Yeah." The butter pecan lid was conquered with much more aggression.

"At school?"

"Yeah. She's also at Teacher's College, but she is studying education not nutrition."

"How did you meet her?"

Strawberry-blond hair shimmering, getting darker at the roots with the sweat of an Indian summer; the lightest of pink legs sprawled along the side steps, sprawled themselves with almost-white freckles— "What a place to hide on such a beautiful day." "Well, where else can I honestly pretend I am reading and still be outdoors?"— legs that moved against her brown skirt, opening ever so slightly, revealing a shadow as she laughed into the sun when he asked if he could join her later in this hiding spot; he also had some reading he needed to pretend to do…

"At school, Mom." *I already said that.*

"I see. How old is she?"

Why does it matter? "I don't know; twenty-three, I guess." He stuffed an angry helping of butter pecan into his mouth, saving it from falling off the spoon.

"Does this girl have a name?"

"I think I would put the vanilla with the apple pie, and go double pecans for the other one." He got up, frustrated, confused about his inability to explain the sheer magnitude of this meeting. He walked out of the kitchen thinking, *Why am I so angry, I want to hit her?* And heard himself ask, "Who in here wants dessert?"

He started to take count, but Inise took over, asking, practically over her shoulder in her need for the kitchen, "Who wants it *ala mode?*"

Mac escaped to the toilet room, but in the absence of any urine, he found himself, against all the best intentions, long-faced, openmouthed, squeezing around blackheads.

The phone sirened. Mac stared at his freshly red nose. *It could be her.*

"Well, yes, dear; happy holidays to you too; can I ask who is calling? Georgia? MAA'AC! It's Geeoorgia."

Shit. Mom can't be talking to Georgia. Ughh. I can't enter the kitchen with my nose looking like this.

His fingernail imprints were refusing to fill in. "I'll take it upstairs," coolly calmly, out the bathroom, passing the kitchen fast, face down, turning, taking as many stairs as possible with one stride, *how many words can Mom get in before I—*

"It is very thoughtful of you to call. Are you having a good holiday?…Still at school! That's no good. And Mac said you were studying to be a teacher? How nice."

"Mom, I got it." *Please just shut up. She doesn't need to know I've been talking about her!*

"OK, well next year I hope you come here and have a proper Christmas." Mac heard Inise snort as his mother hung up the phone.

His stature was swallowed by the softness of his parents' bed, where he sat hunched into the phone, like an adolescent trying to escape. "Hey."

"Hey! Merry Christmas! You are lucky to be out of the city; it is really coming down…" Her voice was mutated by the wires but somewhere in there, in the tempo of her words, was Georgia.

"Really?" He imagined watching it together, from the window of her apartment, him gathering the undercut of her hair against her nape and kissing that small bone at the top of her spine. He found his hand in his crotch and reminded the unruly extremity about the open door. He moved the hand abruptly but didn't know where to place it instead. "I miss you."

She made a miniscule sound of relief. "I miss you too. I wasn't sure if I should call, but then I figured what was the point of you giving me your number, if I shouldn't call."

"You figured right." She was smiling; he just knew it, maybe running her hand over the frost on the pane, maybe thinking of running her fingers over something else...

"I finished my present for you today," she hinted, aiming to be seductive, trying to create mystery.

Present? Shit. "But you said you and your *über*-intellectual parents don't celebrate Christmas."

Giggling, it was not the game she was looking for, but still fun. "Yep, 'every day is a holiday.' But I wanted to make you a surprise."

"Well as long as it is an everyday-holiday surprise, not a Christmas surprise." *I can find an everyday surprise, or hell, perform an everyday surprise, but Christmas surprises, that's heavy.* "So what is it?"

"Can't tell you." She laughed; here was the game she was after.

54

"Is it coal?"

"No. You've been a very good boy this year, I think."

"Sexy lingerie?"

"For you to wear or for me?"

"Hey, don't do that; don't make me think of myself in lingerie. I mean, it's Christmas and all."

"So not Christmas, but on other days?" A skimming tease, her hair must be flipping a little, brushing her shoulder even.

"Never, that's disgusting; now you in lingerie..." *what kind would it be...Playboy* versions catalogued through his mind, all seeming perfect to take off her..."Is that what the surprise is? Lingerie!"

"No." She laughed. "Sorry."

"Awhh. Give me a clue."

"I made it."

"You made it. Can it fit into a shoe box?"

"I dun'no-o," sing-song refrain: I caan't teell you, but I will tell you that, "I miss you." He heard the "you" as a pucker followed by a grin.

"I miss you too." Two puckers, and the same stupid grin.

Chapter Ten

"So where are you headed?"

The question reverberated unattended, as he relinquished himself to his chair after Jerk Daniels' defeat. *This seat cost as much as Jerk. Am I missing the karmic humor?*

"Uhhh, what? Boston?" *Just like you, lady, this bus is express.*

"So what do you do for a living?"

This again. "I stuff vitamins down the throats of children." *Or tell other people to.*

"Oh how interesting; my daughter is about your age, and she is a nurse."

"I'm not a nurse." He refused to make eye contact. *Will she get the point?*

"Oh, well, she loves the doctors."

"I am not a doctor."

"Umm, OK, it still sounds a little like what my Ellie does. Are you married?"

Georgia in white gauze, just her face, fleeting, *what could it have been like…*"No."

"You going home for the holidays?"

"Ya." Georgia's face turned from the wedding bough to be lit up by miniature bulbs, red and green.

"So what did you get your mother for Christmas?"

The gauze morphed into the short bob of his mother, and the smile broadened into an entrained grin. All of Georgia was lost. "Not sure yet." He let it out hard.

"Well, why not!"

"I was busy at work."

"Too busy with vitamins to get your mother a present?"

"Apparently."

"Well, Ellie finds the time."

"I'm sure she does," he said, feigning sleep, trying to recapture the images of the girl, the transient expressions, the pink skin, the freckles, the halo of blond bangs.

The bus slowed to pull into the Boston bus station. The deceleration caused everyone to stand and rummage at the overhead shelf, priming themselves for the race that was about to begin; ready, set…Using the loudspeaker as backup, Bus-Madam berated them to stay in their seats until the bus was no longer moving, but she did it just as she was parking and coming to a full stop anyway. There was a little passenger hiccup, and then everyone was at the shelf again, standing, waiting, still waiting, to get off. The woman at his shoulder, knocked him with her knuckles, and pointed out the window.

"There's my Ellie! Isn't she beautiful. You will have to come meet her and tell her what you do."

"Look, I have a girlfriend, OK?"

"Well, that's not, well, I—"

I couldn't have waited until this line was moving before I said that? Awkward, awkward, pretend you have already parted ways…

The woman sat back down, and poured attention on the bow at the reindeer's antlers. Her hand was trembling a bit.

Aww, man, now I feel bad. "It was nice talking to you, and I am sure Ellie is a catch, but my girlfriend just wouldn't approve." *Asshole, wake up. You don't have a girlfriend, she is gone, remember? Even Ria left you.*

The line was moving, *you're gonna do it, aren't ya; yep, too tired not to.* "I hope you and Ellie have a nice holiday."

She didn't look up and the aisle train carried him away.

Once outside, he tried to look distracted by focusing on the luggage man tossing bags over his shoulder as if he was shoveling snow. Mac found his own bag on the pavement, shouldered it, and swung past Ellie, before they could be introduced, before her mother could tattle about how some guy, that guy, was so rude. Ellie, *it figures*, really wasn't that bad. Perhaps a bit too thin but kinda cute. She even looked a little stressed to see her mother, which he could appreciate, but Mac kept moving; there was no clean slate on this one. He moved through the glass doors and into the round robin of donuts, coffee, and ticket agents. An impersonal clock read 4:45.

Damn she drove fast. I'm actually gone make it there.

Chapter Eleven

Saturday morning. It was already late: nine o'clock. The Cambodian sun was rising fast. But somehow the world seemed less bleak today. He felt more like himself. He wanted to explore, maybe even practice his Khmer. Something he hadn't been inspired to do in years.

He left his house, stepping out into the mud. The city's streets were sweaty with dust and exhaust. Bicycles flew past. And motorcycles honked English, offering him a ride. He smiled, but his head shook "no thanks," a refusal that he would repeat fifty times in the next few hours.

He wanted to walk and slowly rediscover his neighborhood. His office was only down this wide road, near the promenade area, a road and area he knew by heart, but what about the unpaved paths? He took an abrupt turn and dodged a motorcyclist.

Maybe they are trying to run me over, so they can offer a ride to the hospital. He laughed to himself. He towered over everyone in the street. How could he feel even slightly threatened?

He spotted an open-air market ahead. The roof was created from blue tarps and plastic bags, slung from bamboo. Mac bumped into a pole as soon as he tried to properly enter, and the ceiling announced his presence with a tremor. He slouched to a three-quarters height to accommodate the low ceiling.

Underneath the makeshift umbrellas, women squatted near the ground. They fanned flies from open cuts of meat and heads of fish, or rearranged produce to place the most seductive samples on top. Babies were tended and shared as the favored entertainment. The women with recognizable snacks—donuts, peanuts, fruit—waved him over; the others, after one long look, ignored him.

On the far side, near the return of sunshine, phallic eggplants huddled against pregnant onions. Their saleswoman laughed openly at the flirtations of a woman crouching with gossip. The gossiper's shoulder supported a long stick, which, if she were to stand, gravity would have weighted with the help of two baskets of miniature bananas. The bunches groped at her breasts, but she was too absorbed in her story to pay them much notice. Creasing her eyes at the woman with the onions, she only slapped at the breast-feeders absent-mindedly.

To the left of them, a boy squatted on a piece of cardboard that had been heroically placed atop a small mountain of durian. The melon-sized fruits, heavy and thorned in peel and odor, were stacked like Legos, catching one another with their spines. The boy, balanced on his calves, looks quite stable as he used a cleaver to crack open a shell. His customer was plump in dirty trousers; her shirt boasted Mickey Mouse on its pocket. The succulent durian embryo was received in Styrofoam. The woman looked hypnotized by its flesh and her daughter, a long pull

60

of taffy from the mother's side, suddenly bent closer, inspecting, smelling, wanting a taste now.

Cups and bowls had gathered behind the piles of produce. Glasses of iced tea and sugar cane juice, bowls with last sticks of wet noodles, or traces of rice. Breakfast was just finishing, and vendors hunched their way through to collect the dishes and make a last sale. Kids played assistant to their mothers by fetching a late morning's treat. All the empties reminded Mac that he owed himself a coffee.

From the pungency under the tarps, he could see another shaded area, separated from the market by a stripe of sunlight. It was shade made by a piece of corrugated scrap metal, which strut over dry benches and a wood counter. All the markings of a proper café. He had earned a coffee by now: he had already made fun of his foreign ogre-ness to all the staring eyes, when he nearly brought down the roof of the market; he'd already refused, politely of course, rambutan, mango, durian, lychee, fried dough. The top of his back already hurt from the slouching under the low tarps, even if he was still enchanted with the colors, voices, and baskets, giving and collecting their way through the mud.

He escaped to the bewildered squint of the café's mistress. Thick espresso arrived over a layer of sweetened and condensed milk. A spoon turned the shot glass into a hot liquid candy bar. Sipping, he looked around the table. She had forgotten something. With a gesture, he proudly proved that he wasn't just some passing tourist; he too wanted the green tea back. A kettle filled a smeared highball glass and he used the hot tea to cleanse his palette for the next thick sip of coffee. He faced the market, to watch the shadows, and to sweat his own moisture into the scene.

A black pair of mid-calf pants walked along the edge of an umbrella he had recently ducked. Clutched against the waist was a woven plastic bag in what used-to-be white. A turquoise shirt, a smart button-down, hugged a miniscule frame. Its collar accepted the corners of a purple kerchief tied over the hair and under a chin. It looked like her, but the sunglasses made it hard to be sure.

The girl looked out of place, perhaps on purpose. But she chatted glibly with the onion woman, and nodded at the banana gossiper, with a politeness suggesting an awareness of her youth. She shrugged and gestured at the boy atop the durian, and then broke into shamefaced laughter. The laugher's posture, the throw of her head, assured Mac. It had to be her. The girl with the musical hair. He turned around to hand a dollar to a girl checking on the level of the kettle, causing both her and her mother to scurry around, looking for enough riel to make change, while he readied for flight, watching Ria poke and sniff durian. She had already picked one, had it peeled, Stryofoamed and bagged, before his change was found.

He caught her at a bicycle he hadn't noticed.

"Hey!" he shouted, a little too loud, as he ran up to her.

Startled, she looked embarrassed to see him. As he got closer, he saw little threads coming out of the turquoise seams. The top button was missing, and the pants were faded into soft cotton thinness, even a little sheer in the knees and butt. Her sunglasses followed their job requirement and said nothing, but her mouth was in turmoil. "Oh, hi," it managed.

In the pause that followed, Mac realized he had nothing to say.

The turmoil at her mouth was passed up to the delicate curve between her brows. "I am sorry I am so stinky with all this durian."

"I actually don't mind durian smell." *See, I am not your average Westerner.* "Just surprised to see you here."

And wow, that durian stank; its sweet smoke wafted around her bicycle in the drama of the morning heat. Ria wanted to escape and come back looking, and smelling, better. She looked down, searching the basket for her confidence.

Mac finally found something worth saying. "Had fun meeting you last night; should do it again sometime?" His voice rose too much at the end; *did I just sound like a girl?*

His awkwardness helped her find the lost item. "Sure." She faced him with a polished smile.

He collected her number on the back of his business card, and she fled the scene, her heels pushing green flip-flops against pedals. As her delicate torso rode away, one knee rose up to cross politely over the other, baring long indents around an anklebone. The fingered card slipped back into a slit in his wallet; its leather felt hotter than usual all day.

He offered to pick her up, but she insisted they would meet him there. "They." He'd never hated a pronoun so much.

The restaurant, large and open air, with a patio over the river, was farther from the city than he expected and flanked by noisier clones. All of three restaurants seem pretty empty, but the karaoke blasting from the farther one and the live cover band from the previous one were trying to drown out their solitude. The chosen restaurant's specialty was hot pot soup. That had been his guise, "Where's the best hot pot soup," putting the wheels in motion that led to this very spot.

They, Chanroth and Ria, arrived together on a motorcycle. The intimacy of their arrival, her seated sidesaddle, leaning close to Chanroth, her breast brushing his back, hands around his waist, was all flung away as soon as he stopped. She hopped off and looked only at Mac as Chanroth dealt with the key and kickstand. Mac was pleased to see Chanroth have to trail after her, and made a point to greet them separately.

They sat outside, and in the breeze of noise coming from the other two restaurants, Mac joked how they got to hear two performances from their table and didn't have to pay the cover for either. Chanroth stared wistfully along the riverside, at the other patio bedecked with performers, but diplomatically contributed something about it being easier to talk here; he was glad for the opportunity to practice his English.

Prepubescent waitresses floated among the clash of songs like dissatisfied butterflies—who long to be beauty contestants. Each girl wore a sash over a single shoulder and its mock silk jingled a beer slogan. Six hovered around Mac, giving him a glass, a bottle of water, a cup of ice, a beer, a glass for the beer, ice for the beer, giggles. Chanroth pretended not to notice and gruffly ordered for them all.

Fried peanuts arrived mixed with browned garlic slices. And then a pot filled with broth was plugged into the table. It was accompanied by containers of salt, sugar, lime, pink fish paste, chopped chili floating in vinegar. Three bowls and a ladle. Everyone sat still, waiting. Platters arrived with tofu, sliced meat, raw egg, yellow noodles, bean sprouts. Chanroth got everything started in the pot as two more plates arrived. Pork pieces, in a thick black oyster sauce, were freckled by chili pepper seeds, and okra fingers sautéed dormant. Bowls of rice sat stubbornly in front of them all. Ria picked up her chopsticks, while Mac clutched his spoon. They were all starving and agreed on a universal truth: food is good.

Mac was curious about their childhoods. He couldn't help himself. But they skirted any unpleasantries. Turns out that poor agrarian Cambodian children do the same water-splashing, bug-torturing, activities of a middle-class Massachusetts boy.

Talk of the past sputtered to a halt, so Mac turned to the present. "That's a nice bike you got there."

"It's a friend's. But I am getting a car soon—" Chanroth broke off.

Ria rescued the sentence, and bragged for her friend about his new fancy job. His English and French had earned him a position driving for an international organization. It was really a great job. And they would keep him forever, she was sure. They would even provide him with money for health care and use of the vehicle in his free time. But Chanroth didn't look up. His face turned red and he excused himself to the bathroom.

"And what about you? What are your plans for after graduation?"

"Oh, I am supposed to get married." She laughed. "But I keep telling my father I am too young."

"Where's your father?"

"He's at Angkor. He opened a guesthouse there in Siem Reap when we came back from Thailand."

"That was smart. Is the rest of your family there too?"

"No, only my father and I went to Thailand."

"Oh." He knew the rest of the story without asking. He had heard many variations on it from countless Cambodians. The tone was even the same, the happy other side of the mask, the convex curves over the concave ripples of survivor's guilt...

Spring 1970. A right-wing general, backed by the United States, deposed and replaced a popular king. Uncertainty, bombing, and hardship followed, fueling the previously feeble growth of the communist underground over the next five years. The ex-king briefly gave the communists his backing, and the insurgency swelled. Civil war began. The insurgency gained the upper hand, holding the majority of the country, but the general had access to US weaponry.

On April 12, 1975, America abandoned ship. Operation Eagle Pull: The communists will win; save the Americans. All US support was stopped at once, from critical yet covert military assistance to humanitarian aid, with personnel evacuations completed by helicopter. A vacuum was left in their wake. Five days passed.

And then it all happened in twelve hours. April 17. Year Zero. War was over. The Khmer Rouge was in control. Celebration, liberation, followed by complete evacuation of the capital city. You just have to leave for a few days, residents were told; the Americans plan to bomb Phnom Penh, get out. You will be safe in the countryside.

Despite the calm orders, the exhausted, but armed, men-in-black frightened many, including Ria's father. There were upper-circle rumors of an ideology that ringed with hatred for personal property and education. An engineering professor, he went home early that day, and the decision was made in a quarter of an hour. He would leave for Thailand, and ride out this confusion, to sneak back in later, in a few days, when the city returned to normal. Just to be safe, on his return, he would dress as a peasant. They could afford for him to bring one with him; their only daughter seemed the natural choice.

Escaping over the border was likely a dark blur of caves, stewed leaves, and gunshots. Trauma would have washed away much of the little girl's memory of life before.

But, inside Cambodia, horror beyond any expectation ensued. Suggestions that the urban evacuations were temporary were blatant lies. Instead, bloodbaths systematically "cleansed" the populace of the "elite," such as people who wore glasses or knew more than one language. Only farmers were considered worthy citizens. Schooling was a sin deserving of death. Ownership was redefined as theft, and communal farming began. And failed. Paranoia beset leader Pol Pot, and orderly genocide ensued.

66

Perhaps there was a letter from her mother, a hazy letter about hard work and soups made with bark and miniature worms, a haze that hesitated to reveal the swollen bellies of sons, who were dropping away to the flies. Smuggled, at great risk, into the border camp, such a letter would have filled a night with a father's pounding rage. While a little girl proved herself to be a horrible, horrible person by being so glad not to be with her mother and brothers, but instead to be with her father, where she could have a bowl of steaming white rice. In the salt of her father's sobs, she ate. The letter's details were swallowed like tiny rocks among the polished rice, to sit at the bottom of her belly, never to be metabolized, while she took another scoop out of the Thai pot, looking elsewhere, anywhere, and stuffing her mouth, eating for her brothers too, and adding more and more chili to be punished by its burn.

There was no family left when they returned. The stones in her belly were her only reminders....

Her insect-catching stories had included brothers; Mac wondered how many, but didn't ask.

Chanroth returned, but Mac continued addressing Ria. "So, will you go stay in Siem Reap?"

"My school friends are here in Phnom Penh."

"Besides, what is there to do at Angkor other than talk to Westerners?" Chanroth glared.

"We like the city. We like the cafes and stuff." She went on trying to describe Phnom Penh as if it was the Paris she had seen in photographs. And, of course, there were similarities in architecture—wide boulevards, romantic verandas, shutter-clapped windows, cobbled sidewalks, boutiques, large public spaces—but crumbling, neglected, dissipating. Still, somehow, Chanroth and Ria saw Paris in the cloud of decay and pollution that was Phnom Penh.

They retaliated with questions about the United States. Both dreamt of going someday; a dream that was worse than impossible, with its miniscule itch of hope. Mac tried to trace the lines of a quaint New England town in the clouds of their imagination. But "quaint" didn't translate, and Mac didn't really believe in its accuracy anyway. Perhaps they were imagining something out of a sitcom. Monolithic skyscrapers, however, found easy saliency. They had seen plenty of movies.

Suddenly, the sky cracked open. Rain gushed over the awning as a waitress tallied the accumulation of side plates, empty beer mugs, and bottles of water onto their bill. Mac's shoulders steamed from the broth's galingale and lemongrass. "Thanks for such a good recommendation."

"We usually go next door for the music, but the food is better here."

The floor was gently flooding. Water was seeping into Mac's shoes. A stroke of genius. "So can I offer you two a ride?"

"Well, I have my motorbike here."

I know. "Oh, well, Ria, can I at least get you home dry?"

"I am staying with Chanroth."

"Well, I can easily drop you off there; my driver is waiting for me in the parking lot."

Chanroth looked at the table.

Chapter Twelve

From the bus station's smeared doors, he found himself back outside, met by a temperature drop of forty degrees.

All right; I give up.

Back indoors, he unzipped the duffel bag and rummaged for his coat. Ellie and her mother passed by, or at least his peripheral vision briefly held nurse's shoes and a bag holding a taunting reindeer. Mac found his coat but kept rummaging while they passed, eyes to the ground, hunched and concentrated, *why do old people have to walk so slow; where are my gloves?*

At last, he felt safe enough to start the zippering process. He stood and glanced at Ellie helping her mother into a cab, while he put his coat on with great care, looking at each sleeve like it was the first time he had gotten dressed. And they were off. Off to have lots of reindeer cheer. And to fortify their family against people like him.

Let's go subject mine to me. He swung back out the door and a taxi driver, with a belly bulging from the V of a bottom-zippered leather jacket, approached, confidently reaching for Mac's bag. "Need a ride?"

"Ya."

Before he knew it, he felt about four years old again, trailing after some big man, who was carrying all his stuff for him, and was the sole bearer of the correct direction. He led Mac through the frosted parking lot to a car. A car, not a taxi. But Mac didn't care. He was too tired to care about a scam at this point.

"How much to Somerville?" he asked out of habit, knowing he would accept almost any price as long as the guy would turn on the heat. He told him as much.

"You cold, brother?"

"Freezing."

"Well, all right." The leather jacket practically fell off the driver and was flung into the passenger seat. Short-sleeved, he loaded Mac's bag into the trunk. And then, at last, he started the engine and the heater, which blew nothing but cold air for at least five minutes.

Finally, *ah there's that smell of baked air*, gristled with the security of warmth. Memories of cold winter nights, soon to become warm, a clanking heater to the rescue…It clicked the night forward, one notch closer to Christmas morning, as Masterson strained to hear Santa and got only an earful of the heater declaring victory against the cold. *If I sleep, it will come faster. But how will I ever sleep? Will he give me lots? How does he fit under the door? Maybe Santa can become all kinds of sizes, but what about the Raleigh Chopper and all my other presents…can they change sizes too? By themselves, or only when Santa is around?*

Mac settled back and found himself staring at the thick neck of the driver. There was already sweat coming from where hair should be.

70

His eyes moved on to the traffic lights decorated with tinsel wreaths. The windows of several shops were shackled by the letters: H A P P Y * H O L I D A Y S.

Why did I find this anticipation so enjoyable before? Was I just a victim of advertising? I was the fun guy, the exciting generous uncle, brother, son, boyfriend...Where did that guy go? I used to actually worry about people liking their presents. Somebody, brainwash me with holiday spirit, please.

All the stores were dark and locked. The car's digital clock read 5:08.

So glad I am getting there when the festivities are almost over.

Chapter Thirteen

"I am nervous," Georgia admitted.

The taxi came to a full stop on his street. His old street seemed to be aging at a different speed than himself. But it was still his. Even the slush in the gutter seemed familiar. Her mitten, however—in its magenta and green yarn, with her hand stumbling back in, a hand relinquishing his bare skin, to hide from the approaching cold—was stimulation enough to even make the front stoop seem brand new.

Leafing through bills in his wallet, he assured her, "Don't be; they are only going to try to embarrass me; they'll leave you alone."

Out on the street, distracted, she continued, as he picked up the chain of chores and got their suitcases out of the trunk, "But what if they don't like me?"

"How could they not like you?" He smiled. "And if you don't like them, how 'bout we escape to Singapore and Thailand the day after Christmas?"

72

Still distracted, she wanted to carry her own bag, missing his attempt to make her laugh, she at least looked relieved. "I remembered the tickets."

"You should see your sister; she is so happy! Although I think Slade may even be happier than she is." A big helping of lasagna slid from the spatula to the plate, expanding like a deck of cards. It steamed Cate's face as her mother passed the plate to her.

No one commented. Cate squirmed and passed the plate to her husband. Georgia offered, "How far along is she?"

"Just over three months, and all looks good so far. She is just starting to show, but she is planning on hiding it, so they can surprise his family after they open gifts tomorrow. I think it is a wonderful idea—announcing a grandchild at Christmas!"

Pause, pause. "That is kinda a fun idea," Mac suggested to the static air over the table.

"But," his father clarified, "don't let your mother fool you; she is ecstatic to know before Slade's family."

"Well, she's my daughter; of course I should know first." She searched Cate's face with a sidelong glance, but was disappointed. She had always expected Cate to be more about kids than Inise, but it was clear that Cate had no news for her in that regard. "I think this will be a very good thing for the two of them."

"Babies don't save marriages, Mom," Cate spat, and in the same breath, asked, "Georgia, would you like more wine?"

"Uh, sure."

"Mac?"

"Yes, please."

Cate finished the bottle, and turned back to the easiest target, the target that would remind everyone to be on better behavior, "So, Georgia, what subject are you planning to teach after you graduate?"

"Well, I would like to teach elementary school, so I guess all subjects."

"And why elementary school?" Mac's father asked, as he continued searching for a trace of sting in his wife's face.

"Umm, because, I think learning should be fun, and in elementary school they haven't yet decided that school is torture."

"Man, I wish some of my teachers had made school fun. Seems like a hard thing to do though." Greg sounded relieved to have something to contribute.

"But kids are innately curious; you just try to make them curious about the thing you want to teach them, rather than curious about what someone across the room will do if they shoot a spitball at them."

Mac's father laughed, remembering spitballs, now genuinely interested. "And how do you do that?"

"Well, like, you can teach math with stories, or something they will find more interesting than numbers."

"Teaching math with stories?" echoed Greg, scraping a last bit of ricotta from his plate, and then abandoning his fork. He put his hands in his lap and smiled encouragingly.

"Tell 'em about 'numbers as neighbors,'" Mac piped in. "I really like this example."

Georgia's face was red, with wine or embarrassment, Mac couldn't guess, but she continued with a honeyed voice, "Mac is talking about trying to teach complicated subtraction, which I had to do with the class I assisted with last semester. I like to give the numbers characters. The last number in the bottom line is a little kid. And he asks his mom, the last number in the top line, for milk. He drinks it and the amount she has left goes back into the fridge, which is under the equals line."

Georgia swallowed, and looked around the table, breezing the eyes of each adult, trying to keep away the higher voice she used with children. Mac blushed with lust, as he watched her slip into teacher mode. For all the respect he had for her capability with children, he found it adorable that she almost couldn't help herself. The combination was enough to cause a stirring against the seam at his crotch.

"But sometimes the kid asks for more milk than the mom has. So she has to go next door and borrow a surplus of milk, ten to be exact, from her neighbor. The neighbor gives readily, but then when the same scenario repeats in the neighbor's house, when that kid wants more milk, she naturally doesn't go to the lady who came to her; she is sure the milk has already been drunk. She goes to the other neighbor..."

Mac was disappointed that Inise wasn't there. She would have loved this, and encouraged Georgia; he could hear her saying, with sincerity, "Oh that's so cute."

His father filled the void. "Kids nowadays get all the breaks."

"See, kids, when I ran out of groceries, I was just trying to teach you subtraction," his mom preened.

"And when I drank all the milk, I was just trying to learn."

"Oh, so that was what you were up to."

"Yeah. Just wanted to make sure I understood subtraction."

"I should have just given you the grocery bills; that would have taught you plenty about subtraction, without you guzzling all the milk," said Mac's father. Turning to Georgia, he added, "You should have shown up a long time ago, and we would have sorted all this out; you would have saved me a pretty penny."

A pretty penny? The phrase made the four of them laugh. No ugly pennies were worth saving. But two voices were missing. They looked down the table.

Cate had reached for Greg's hand, and then lap, under the table, thinking more about when the next time they could try to get pregnant than listening to Georgia. She covered herself by smiling into the pause and asking mischievously, "So where do you plan to teach?"

"It doesn't really matter to me. Everywhere needs teachers. It is still more than a year away." Georgia directed herself to Cate, but Cate was watching Mac's face.

"But, Mac, you graduate this spring, right?"

Mac nodded. Georgia avoided all peripheral vision.

Over a fluttering sheet, Georgia announced, "I am so full."

Mac pulled it tight and tucked it in the railing support of the couch bed. "That's the way you should feel after a proper Christmas." *Is she as nervous as I am? Sleeping in the same bed under my mother's roof?*

"Well, it is always a good idea to eat well before traveling to Asia. The portions are so tiny over there."

He handed her the edge of another sheet. "The people are so tiny over there."

Georgia laughed. "Singapore and Bangkok probably won't be too bad. But our poor do look fat in comparison, don't they?"

He tossed her a pillow. She caught it and climbed into the bed, the neck of her pajama top hanging provocatively low. "I mean, I remember thinking I was starving, rummaging through empty cupboards for an after-school snack."

She must be nervous; we've had this conversation. Is she nervous about tonight or about the trip? "I know: how come we are so lucky to be born in the United States?"

He climbed in next to her. The metal joints protested loudly, to his disappointment. She pretended not to notice and moved for him to settle, slightly upright, behind her. She put her head on his shoulder.

"It makes me feel bad when I see it; I mean, I didn't do anything to get all the good food and schooling I got growing up. And then I start thinking about the yearly trip for school clothes, fancy dinners, air conditioning, central heating, the fact that I can go anywhere just because I know English…"

"Yeah. The guilt eggs me on too."

"I know it does."

She lifted her head from his chest and fingered the sheet. He watched her mouth soothe into a pout.

A beam creaked somewhere in the house. They both looked up. It was nothing. It had been hours since they heard an actual person, either Cate or Greg, not sure which, exit the guest bedroom to embark on a midnight leak. They had distanced themselves on the couch, straining to hear the flush over their movie, and, finally, to hear the bedroom door close again. The movie's end had left a hole of sound, a vacuum to all their subsequent attempts at conversation.

"I can't believe my mom is going to let us sleep together."

"Yeah, it's pretty cool of her. I wonder what my parents would do. I wonder if all their progressiveness would break down over something like this."

"Well, I guess, it is kind of a compromise. Did you notice she refused to call it a couch *bed*? It's like, as long as it is still a couch, it doesn't really matter that we're not married."

"It's probably that whole 'still out in public' thing."

"Yeah, like we are still being chaperoned or something."

"But sometimes being out in public can be half the fun," she said, looking down at the sheet covering them both.

Mac felt a timid figure eight swirling along his lower thigh. He stretched his arm around her, to clasp the far shoulder with his palm, gently, as if it was a fruit he wanted to pick without bruising. With the scent from her skin, he made a decision.

He bent into her face, "I don't think anyone will see if I..."

Her lips were sticky with a flavored Chapstick and melted apart quickly with the beckon of a hot tongue. Her mouth felt like summer and he ran a hand through the sprinkler of her hair. The bitten tips of her fingers chased each other up his inner thigh, and ducked into the tunnel of his shorts.

He gasped into her mouth and they both opened their eyes. Hers had gone green and wet; they invited his in for a swim. Fumbling through the leg opening of his shorts, her hand inched toward his balls, stroking the hairs, fingering, playing...The angle of her wrist released, and the hand went out and over his shorts, just brushing his hard shaft. "I don't think anyone will see if I..." an echo as she conquered the elastic band and grabbed hold.

The strokes were gentle and loose. A finger brush of acknowledgment to the balls, before moving back up along the veins of the shaft. Feathered curiosity around the head, the tiny hole, the rim, the soft flesh in between, and then back to the hard rod. He gave her some of his moistness and the strokes became firmer, fantastically rhythmic, while his eyes poured into her unfailing stare.

He blinked heavily and she kissed his face with calm approval, as her hand hastened under the sheet. His head fell back, as if accepting a scalding agony. He grimaced, trying to be quiet, as all sensation shrunk, all gravity collapsed, into one exploding sun. Debris was collected by her hand and by the elastic solar system.

He sighed against his lip and she hovered above, shifting to stroke his face with her clean hand. Shivers passed over his body. Before lying back, she kissed his T-shirted shoulder. The couch bed creaked. He smiled at the sound with his eyes closed. On their backs, side-by-side, he could not open his eyes, so deep was the reverberation, but his hand restlessly maneuvered through the sheet folds to find her pajamas. It spidered up her leg and under the waistband, to find her seed already licked by juice.

As he intensified the pulse, her rising breath made his own chest warm with excitement. He folded to a fetal position, switching to his right hand, for more suppleness, and she folded too, spooning against him, feeling him stirring, slightly hard again, into her buttocks. The bed creaked once more. She bit into the pillow as his finger increased its speed. Heat baked the acidic honey between her thighs. Its flame flickered, coaxed, teased, until, with a muffled squeal, the seed burst and unfurled forth.

There seemed to be a soft rocking as he cupped his palm against her secret hair. Slowly, the tension in her shoulders evaporated. She unclenched the pillow. He pulled his hand out from her pajama bottoms. Wrapped as a fist, it pushed against the flannel between her breasts. She pulled deeper into his curve, pressing the back of her body into the front of his, from ankle to shoulder. His breath passed over her neck to join hers. They were both still shaking some. They fell asleep in the glow of their volley.

Chapter Fourteen

As the car filled with dry heat, Mac's nose thawed enough to run. The "car service" driver made small talk, continuing to refer to him as "brother," hoping to make an extra tip. Mac was mostly unresponsive; he contributed occasional sniffles.

They passed a school ground, frozen in mid-construction. It was a scene that would have gotten Georgia all excited. She liked parks, golf courses, playgrounds, gardens—really any manicured outdoor space— seeing all her nature vs. nurture quandaries debated in their short grasses and defined shrubs. Mac imagined her looking at this static school ground and suddenly musing about "latent potential" vs. "critical periods." He sniveled distractedly at the driver's question about the radio, as he watched a cardinal padding the snow...

"You remind me of a heron today," she shouted across a pond in an immaculately designed Singapore park, the day before they continued on to Thailand.

"A heron?"

"Ya." She clamored down the side of a boulder, purposely placed for climbing.

He watched, not so much her exactly, but his world with her in it. She was reflected not only in the pond but in every color and shadow of the cultivated trees and blossoms, meandering tourists, and Singaporeans…"Why is that?"

"You look like you could stand like that forever."

Like this? Watching you, having fun? "I plan to."

"Aww, even a heron's gotta move sometimes."

"Why? It is nice here." He watched her hips approach.

"Don't know really." She took a sudden turn and sat in the grass next to the pond. He mimicked her movement. She threw a tiny pebble into the water, her face echoing the pond with a ripple of thought. Suddenly, she exclaimed, "OK, you've convinced me: let's stay here forever."

"Sounds good to me. But what about Thailand?"

"Oh yeah. Well, maybe it can come here too."

"Here, Bangkok; here, boy," Mac whistled and slapped his thigh.

She turned to him to share her laugh. The day in the sun had spread freckles across her nose, but among all their speckled youth, her eyes sat contradicting them with a hurried search for time. "Where you gonna go next year?"

"Well, if I get this job in Cambodia, that would be my first choice." Emerging from thirty years of civil war, not to mention the four years of genocide targeting the educated, leaving only fifty doctors in the entire country…Starting over, thousands of refugees pouring in from stagnant border camps, which they have called home for over a decade…Only two years after the UN-held election, a need to rebuild at every level, from personal trauma to families reuniting under the anger of abandonment…From paving roads over land mines, to basic health services…What an opportunity to actually be of service.

"But that's not here," she pointed to her knee. She meant to point to her lips, but she lost courage.

"I know; but maybe, after you graduate…here can come there too?" he said, feeling a sense of panic arise, as if his want might be too big.

She smiled, a crescent of light, and lifted to plant her lips on his. Slipping her hand into his, she faced the pond again, and leaned her head on his upper arm. With the other hand, she grabbed a bigger pebble. It kerplunked in the water with a giddy splash…

The light dimmed as Mac looked at the car window, instead of out of it. He noticed frost on the humming, ill-fitted glass; it looked like a spider web. *I'm really more of a spider, than a heron.*

Chapter Fifteen

Cambodia's paved road petered out. At the provincial office, they stopped the jeep. Masterson climbed out of the backseat. The two medics, from the kingdom's Ministry of Health, examined him guardedly as he straightened to a foot taller than both of them. He tried to stoop as he accepted a helmet. They were switching to motorbikes to make use of the small paths. He was warned again of landmines. He nodded; he knew not to venture into the grass.

Vibrations purred against his butt as he tried to watch the dirt, mud, and rocks, and still take in the rice paddies, checkering between green and mirror-flooded squares. Most of the scene was brand new to him. Among gardens and rounded leaves, homes appeared in clumps of gray, constructed of corrugated aluminum, unfinished planks, and layer upon layer of dried palm leaves.

Around noon, they arrived at a roadside food stall. Masterson mutely followed the pantomimes of the medics. He ducked under the overhang and, still mimicking, pointed to one of the open pots of stews in various colors and consistencies. He was given a rather bland bit of tripe in yellow sauce, a huge egg, and tons of rice. Between themselves, the two medics fussed anxiously about him, forgetting he could speak some Khmer, afraid that he wouldn't like the food. So he ate with gusto. And every time he was about to finish his rice, the stall owner gave him another scoop.

A woman came in from the road, in a checkered shirt and flowered sarong. Her face was creased darkly with sunshine, and she carried a large bowl teeming with blackness. Kacham's eyes lit up, so Mac took a better look. The woman approached the table, meekly advertising her deep-fried spiders. Kacham bought a full bag.

"You want to try?" Kacham tittered, looking embarrassed.

Masterson couldn't help but grimace, but he also needed to prove himself. He took one. The creature was the width of his palm! He broke off a toothpick-sized leg and found it crispy and tasting of teriyaki. Kacham explained that one is supposed to eat the whole thing at once, head and all. Mac closed his eyes and popped the round body parts in as well. They exploded with oil and Mac didn't bother to cloak his shiver. The medics laughed heartily as he opened his eyes with a grin.

Upon arrival, a fluttery, but vivid, village health volunteer, chosen for her popularity and literacy, greeted them next to a broken sugar-palm juicer. Lounging in the dried sugar, a black butterfly welcomed them with only a yawn of her white tail and red legs.

The woman offered them chairs in the overhang's shade and sat cross-legged on a slotted table, along with a few curious onlookers. With a bright smile, and a nervous giggle, she gave the medics her list of mothers and children, and promised to help gather them to the vaccination site the next day.

84

By this time, more people had come to stare. Masterson was a particular curiosity, but the fellow Cambodian visitors were also of interest. The medics were vaguely familiar; they lived in the nearby town, and worked in the closest health center. But their outdated button-down shirts and cheap jeans looked out of place among the villagers' head wraps, sarongs, and outfits. Boasting teddy-bear motifs, matching pajama pantsuits in thin cotton seemed to make especially proud daytime wear among the adults. Tiny girls looked like gypsy spirits with bare chests and full skirts, while sisters, just a few years older, accessorized their hips with infant siblings. Ubiquitous rubber flip-flops cushioned heels with dignity, as large *kramas,* in red-and-white checkers, draped over shoulders, or fastened around heads, waists, babies. Stretched over newly budding breasts, a turquoise T-shirt read, in English, "The best sauce is hunger in the world." A cartoon pig sat over the words, clutching fork and knife.

The medics explained to their audience, they would be back tomorrow to start the vaccinations. They would be staying several days, using this main village as a base to approach smaller clusters of homes. Gratitude was heaped on the villagers. The village health volunteer blushed.

Walking back to their accommodations, the medics told Mac that he would be handing out paracetamol, a fever reducer, as well as vitamin A. There was a concern that parents would become suspicious of vaccinations if a chance fever resulted, no matter how temporary or innocuous it was.

Feeling like just an extra set of hands, Masterson started expounding on the questionnaire he had brought to facilitate his organization's field research. It had a few questions for each mother, such as "How many people in your household can't see after dark?" or, equivalently, "How many are 'evening chickens?'" But much of it relied on simple observation, like counting the number of people with foamy spots in their eyes.

They nodded at him, aware of his organization's desire to "assess the problem." They had been briefed on how easy it was to diagnose a community with vitamin A deficiency, or, to those who are savvy, VAD. One or two cases of night blindness were sufficient to announce a communitywide health problem.

But Masterson was mired in mechanism. He hastened to show that he knew as much as they did. "You're right; VAD is easy to assess. Because long before it affects the eyes, it affects the immune system. I used to think it was only for vision, but," he continued, as if reciting his textbook, "it is also needed by the skin, the inside of the mouth, the lining of the digestive and respiratory tracts, and lots of other stuff, which I am sure you both know," but which Masterson himself was failing to remember in the moment's humidity. He raised his voice, adding emotion to his pace. "People with VAD aren't just prone to blindness; they are prone to almost any and every infection."

Radath, one of the medics, reacted, "I think, what it really comes down to is that in vitamin-deficient villages, people are just sick for longer. And when they get sick, they can't work in their fields. They lose crop sales that season, and can't afford to eat anything other than rice. Which only makes them all the more sickly. I often think of it as a circle that just keeps going faster. Their children never get healthy, and they miss out on a lot of school." She made a gesture indicating that the lack of education is part of the spiral. And then her hand cut short. "Many die. But, understandably, people blame the death on measles, diarrhea, or bad karma. They don't blame it on malnutrition."

"But this connection is the big break for vitamin A capsules." Masterson spouted the excitement of having his organization receive new funding. As a result, this pilot project, to fight child mortality with cheap

86

VA capsules, was being undertaken to "prove" coverage would be more extensive if VA it was included with vaccination efforts.

The two nodded at him again, this time with both agreement and fatigue. They had reached their rooms. Kacham explained that, in general, it would be best if Masterson headed the line with his questionnaire, before the kids started crying from the shots. Masterson beamingly accepted his assignment, and started thinking about the next day.

The couple postured about, politely hovering at his door. Finally, they asked if he would be OK alone until morning. Assured, they say good night.

It was their third morning in the village, and Masterson had woken up a half hour late. He made his way to the site alone, confident that his tardiness would not be reprimanded. Perhaps, he was finally adapting to the pace of life here.

On either side of the road, occasional huts hovered on stilts, high enough for people to rest underneath in the shade. Wet bras and sarongs were hung from spaces between floorboards, as were occasional hammocks with child. The grass in the surrounding rice paddies was greener than any green he thought possible. *How can something that comes from such color be devoid of so many vitamins?*

It was not yet nine but the air was already caked with mud and sweat. Humans and water buffalo plodded barefoot through the paddies, wet up to mid-calf. Children shouted for school pens, their voices lining the road. Some circled and taunted him, asking for money for milk.

Ahead of him was an enticing butt, wrapped firmly in a sarong. It swayed gently to the bell around a buffalo's neck. She had a stake and rope in hand, and the long-lashed mud-beast trotted behind. For a moment, Masterson also felt leashed by the sway in the sarong.

Passing chickens pruning in a nearby puddle and toddlers, he reached the vaccination post. One of the medics was already setting up, having just arrived with the cooler of ice. Masterson silently began to help and unpacked plastic baggies of vitamin A supplements. *The most cost-effective health intervention in the world,* he mimicked the reports. Absent-mindedly, he gently squeezed the soft capsules.

They expected many kids today. Yesterday's afternoon visit, the first this trip, discovered a child being kept home with a bad case of measles. His parents thought it was dangerous to let his rash see sunshine, or so Mac gathered. The rest of the children, it was arranged, would be taken to the post this morning.

He moved to a low stool and stacked yellow cards against the table. He would hand out the health cards in hope of starting some kind of record, to be held by the child's mother, of vaccinations and supplementation. Kacham handed him the tally sheet. It looked more like a calendar, except, where the ascending dates should be, the village volunteer had written in the number of children to expect in each age group.

In the cluster of a line, one woman was looking particularly stoic. She stared steadily ahead, left arm around an infant cradled against her ribs and right hand directing an eight-year-old toward the makeshift clinic. The boy had his hands on his hips, and his cheeks puffed out. He had been waiting to give Mac a good glare and, once accomplished, he pulled the foot of his brother to whisper loudly, "That is the Frenchie who hurt Daddy with his machine."

His mother told him to close his mouth and forcefully turned him straight ahead with her thumb. She looked nowhere but the top of the door. When it was her turn to answer Mac's questions, she directed the answers at her children.

Mac groped around in his memory. The boy looked familiar. Yesterday's dusk, near his sleeping quarters, twelve boys examining a lighter. One, *this one?* looked up at him fiercely. And then Mac remembered the first night, made dusty already by the memories that had piled up in three eye-opening days:

He had fallen asleep fitfully, after a day of travel, butt sore from the jeep's backseat and back aching from the unaccustomed jostling atop a motorbike, full of hope and pride for the coming morning's efforts, nervous about presenting himself correctly, wanting the people he met to trust—when there was a crash below their quarters and the sound of leaves and wood against metal. Mac rushed down the ladder to the road. He found a man groping against their motorbikes, trying to recollect a large bushel of branches. Mac helped him, asking him where he was going, offering to carry the firewood. But the man only apologized endlessly, with intermittent bows, and worked the enormous load back upon his head. Mac noticed a slight limp, but the bushel, twice as high as the man was wide, stayed impeccably balanced.

The memory was made not so dim, here in the sunshine, where the woman, presumably the man's wife, shaded her baby with her wrap as she waited in a squat for her older son to finish vaccination. Mac found a sterile plastic bag and put in it two red capsules, two full doses of vitamin A, enough to restore the man's night vision. And then abandoned his table as if he was taking a bathroom break. Walking past a row of gossiping mothers, he slipped the bag into her hand and told her they were for her husband, one today and one tomorrow. She folded it into her blouse, nodding, but staring only at her infant. Mac couldn't help but wonder if the baby was having eye problems as well. She hadn't mentioned it. Perhaps she was ashamed. Perhaps it was something else.

Mac returned to his desk, anxious that he should have given some for the mother as well. There was obviously a deficiency in the

89

household…But what if she was pregnant again? VA supplementation in pregnancy could cause birth defects. Did she get some after giving birth? The baby couldn't be more than three months old, too young for routine supplementation. It probably wouldn't have hurt him, but the government was so skittish, it was better for his organization to be cautious. A single incident of toxicity would have brought the whole program to a halt.

The eight-year-old came out of the shade to collect his mother and leave. As she stood up, the mother whispered something into his ear. Hesitantly, the boy turned to Mac and gave a shallow bow, his hands pressed together in front of his chest. His eyes were deflated with confusion, and he turned immediately back to his mother, spilling questions forth.

Masterson continued with the line, smiling to himself, feeling warm that maybe he had helped this man maneuver his way home after dusk. He glanced up to see the threesome making their way down the road, their shadows hiccupping behind them on the uneven dirt. He imagined them presenting the father with the vitamin A. Perhaps the little boy would announce it. But then, in remembering his only interaction with the father, the backs of Mac's arms grew cold.

What if I just damaged what was left of the man's pride? By announcing to his wife, her husband needed some "kid" medicine? Perhaps catching the man in a lie that was already suspected?

Maybe these doses will last long enough and the benefits will outlast the embarrassment. He will need another dose in two weeks. Could I have been able to communicate that? Especially in the time I had to talk to her without raising suspicion among the medics? With too many new questions to ask, he sought distraction in the questionnaire's accumulating data.

Just before lunch, a woman arrived carrying a message from a neighbor. A grandmother's "chicken eyes" made it impossible for her to maneuver kids to the morning post site. The parents were needed by the rice paddies; late December is harvest time. Will "your people" make visits, like they did yesterday?

Mac assured her that the afternoon house-to-house vaccinations would continue that afternoon and took careful note. The village health volunteer had already mentioned this house, but the request was a good sign: the program was no longer being viewed with suspicion. Demand was being created.

When they arrived, the kids were scuffling in the shade between the stilts of the house. They scrambled up the ladder to the one-room hut, and announced the presence of medics and a foreigner to the matriarch. The older sibling returned to the doorway and playfully waved them in.

The structure looked feeble, but, sure enough, it held them all. A grass mat carpeted the floor, and three magazine pictures of US pop stars hovered on one wall. Sleeping pads were folded up in one corner and provisions lined another. Mac's eyes, adjusting to the dim light, followed a sack of rice, a mortar, a kettle, pots, a Folgers coffee can...until they rested on an old woman framed by two small piles of clothes, male and female, and some rummaging children. She sat like a wire hanger bent against the ground. Her foamy eyes were kept shamefully down, as she creaked a bitter "thank you" in English.

Mac gathered the two kids from her side, sitting in front of them so they could still look directly at their grandmother. He gave the eldest of the two a paper cup of water.

Mac started to rip the nipple off the red pill to squeeze the vitamin oil into her mouth. But she gestured something about her height and took the vitamin from him. He managed in Khmer, "It taste not good if chew; just swallow with big water."

The girl laughed at him, but understood. She swallowed like an adult.

The younger one looked at his sister wide-eyed. He whined and squirmed. He put his hands up at Mac.

"What's wrong?" the conversation continued in Khmer.

"He can't swallow like me," boasted his sister.

"That's silly—" *I can just cut the top of and squeeze the oil...*

But the old woman interrupted, "Look at me, look at my eyes, if you say no."

With a choked sob, the boy looked from his grandmother to Mac. He gave a wet blink and offered a cupped palm.

"You can do it, same as sister," Mac coaxed, "with big water."

The boy violently threw his head back with a mouth full of water and vitamin. He gulped and coughed. And then returned to Mac, face red with triumph.

"Good!"

He smiled, spluttering. Under an exaggerated cough, he crumpled the pixie cup in his fist and threw it to the ground. He stomped on it, and looked at Mac and his sister with his chest high and his hands on his hips.

Kacham, with ready vaccinations, applauded, "Wow, what brave children! We've got one more battle for you. Do you think you can do it? First we have to clean up your arms, OK?"

Mac passed Radath the paracetamol syrup as Kacham readied antiseptic wet-naps and pin-prick vaccines. Mac, beaming from the beauty of the boy's pride, was left in the corner with the old woman. She kept her face turned down, focusing on the sounds of her grandchildren at the other side of the room. He wished he knew enough Khmer to
92

describe how the boy's fist had been brought down with such satisfaction. "Your children beautiful," was all he could manage.

"I remember."

As the medics wipe, prick, and reward the children with flattery, Mac gave the woman a capsule and a cup of water. Just as the grandmother was swallowing, Mac caught Radath's eye. She looked the other way.

But later, Radath, lanky with legs and red-black locks, *that's Mrs. Radath, to you, buster,* berated him. She didn't even touch on the most obvious point, the one Mac had drilled into him before leaving Phnom Penh: There-aren't-enough-vitamin-capsules-for-the-entire-community—They-are-specifically-for-those-being-exposed-to-vaccines...

Rather, she berated him, with tears in her eyes and *arak* on her breath, for having the conceit to want to feel good at the end of the day. The arrogance. An impossible vain desire. The need was always, and will always be, greater than the supply. They had to be choosey about who they helped. Helped in the way that would be best for community development in the long run. The older people had fewer years left—

"But they are the children's caretakers."

"I know; you think I don't see that! But, Masterson, the lines have to be drawn somewhere..." The argument was lost to her tears, and she left to find refuge in the shoulder of Kacham.

Chapter Sixteen

Still hoping to inspire generosity in his passenger, the driver settled on a radio station that promised to play hip versions of all his holiday favs.

Mac settled back against the seat and watched the last dregs of Christmas trees being bundled up along the street.

I can't understand why I have to do this. But if I miss it altogether, like that one year…The shadow doesn't fade. No, I will go through some variation of these motions for the rest of my life.

Mac laughed. Really, ever so briefly, laughed aloud. Outside the window, in a churchyard, Paul Revere, the hero who had warned "the British are coming" at the start of the US War of Independence, flailed from atop a bronze horse. Just like he did every day. But this season, someone had strewn a red garland over the statue's shoulder. Mac had briefly mistaken the garland for blood. And it was true, even after a longer look, Paul appeared wounded; his posture slanted backward and his horse looked about to buck.

Mac had always failed to find heroism in this statue. Even as a little kid, Paul had always looked scared to him...

His young teacher roped Masterson's grade-school class around the statue. They were to learn about Revere's midnight ride and follow bits of his route around Boston. She was an extremely tall woman. With her long limbs, she made exaggerated gestures and shouted out the history, trying to compensate for the fog that rises from a field trip. It was a frightening and confusing story. Heroes were not supposed to get caught by the enemy...And if they did get caught, they had to make some phenomenal escape, not simply "let go." And this towering idol looked like he was about to fall off his horse...*This can't be right.*

Not understanding why he should revere Revere, losing faith in his teacher, Masterson had become distracted. He stopped listening and decided for himself. This statue was probably what adults mean when they talk about "shooting the messenger." For the monument seemed more of a warning than an inspiration to young Masterson. He would never be like Revere; he would be a real hero someday. This woman obviously didn't know what she was talking about...

But today, even with the blood-red decoration, an adult Mac found himself more caught up in the statue's static flail, than its fear.

Chapter Seventeen

They took Christmas day off, as it happened to fall on a
Saturday. The second village post was within a day's striking distance
from Angkor, three hours each way.

"It is not really enough time, but it is better than nothing,"
Radath had encouraged.

One of the wonders of the world. With the economic strength of
organized irrigation and labor, a twelfth-century dynasty had celebrated
three hundred years of Hindu-Buddhist unity by building Angkor Wat.
Its architectural feats paid tribute to gods, buddhas, and parents.

"But be careful," she had added.

Last year, peasants had been paid $8,000, and a few water
buffalo, to ambush and murder an American couple as they were
sightseeing among the temple ruins.

The driver, from the provincial office, was plenty game. He had
people he wanted to visit near Angkor. So Mac and he left around 7:00

96

a.m. and, of course, the trip there took a bit longer than the anticipated three hours because a small river that was usually dried out by now was not, and thus they had to wait for a ferry. They arrived at eleven and his driver advised they head back no later than four. The road became more dangerous after dark. Insurgents are nocturnal.

Finally they arrived, and Masterson was dropped off in front of Angkor. Immediately upon leaving the jeep's air conditioning, he felt slapped silly by the heat. He pulled a baseball cap from his knapsack as he glared across a huge moat. There were lotus flowers blooming in the square lake, padding the game of a dozen naked children. The massive stones, which crossed the water, dwarfed them all.

Across the moat, the temple looked like the swollen fortress of a natural kingdom. The center dome was cone shaped in seven successive tapers, surrounded by four smaller versions guarding each direction. He imagined giant bees, hovering, regrouping, planning their next attack, or spoiling themselves in the gold of honey. Palm trees surrounded, beckoning the royal bees' home. The temple's protective walls were adorned with carvings of subjugated humans, and long serpents rode waves down both sides of the bridge. The heads of the snake spirits fanned up with an almost-audible authority; they were laughing at him.

Mac had never seen such a commanding structure. In awe, he started rummaging in his bag for his camera, listening with one ear to the circle of motorcycle taxis that had flocked around him. "No. I am just going to Angkor."

"I take you."

"I don't need a ride; it's right there," he said, laughing, *how lazy do they think tourists are?*

"Not just right there."

"What'dya mean? I can see it." *I'm not falling for your scams...*

The most entrepreneurial of the motorcyclists, the one wearing actual sneakers instead of flip-flops, pulled a map out from the back of his pants. "You here," he pointed to a place on the map, one of many temple-shaped cartoons that was maybe a twentieth of the entire complex labeled Angkor.

"Oh my god, it is huge." The motorcyclists giggled and Mac looked at the sun. *I want to have time to check e-mail, Georgia might...* "All right, you take me?" he gave in, trying to single out this guy with the map over the others standing by. "How much?"

They all started yelling prices.

The wind from the back of the motorcycle was exhilarating and he was giddy with the mysteriousness of the temples. *The world is such a big place; there is so much to see!*

Mac asked Sree to stop intermittently so he could take pictures, trying to juxtapose the green *so green!* rice paddies, grass, wild flowers, and women carrying bushels on their heads, among the humbling grandiosity of the temples. Children chased him, asking him to buy the bottled water and souvenirs, which had just been placed in their hands by their mothers. He sensed he was the Angkor equivalent to America's neighborhood ice-cream man.

Around the next bend, toward the next temple, an enormous face appeared transiently in the rubble. In the humidity, Mac blinked, only to see another illusion, a passing relief, in the cloud of stone. Even with all the wind and chasing and exhilaration, he had to come to a full stop. He clumsily communicated this need to Sree and disembarked equally as clumsily. The motorcyclist waved him on. Wincing into the heat, he passed two small nuns crouched along a newly costumed statue of a reclining Buddha. They fanned intensely at him, inviting him to join
98

them, but he declined, wondering for a second about the history of the creases in their faces.

He climbed up and past, into the temple. Just another bunch of ruins. But, for a moment, another face appeared. His eyes were playing tricks on him; he had been out in the sun too long. And then, there was another face, and another, as he overtook stairs and doorways, and suddenly they were pulsing everywhere around him, five feet tall, and smiling at him, watching his every turn.

Nostrils and eyes were exposed in ripe curves. A hook at the lips forever pushed a cheek up, and out, pregnant with appreciation. A mouth spread, and stretched, with a smile the size of his thigh. He stumbled forward, staring at the enormous faces, not wanting to lose their gaze for even a blink.

But a man waved him out of the sun, into a cavity with a stone *linga*, a symbol of male-female union and the creation of the universe. Mac, reluctantly tearing his eyes from the Bodhisattva expressions, was surprised to see this Hindu symbol. The mumbling man circled the icon and squatted, motioning Mac to follow. In the cool room, light streamed on the linga from a crack in the towering ceiling. The man cupped the light with his hands, and then washed his wrinkles over the phallus. His fingers cupped again at the base, over the *yoni*, and then washed the imaginary fluid over his own face. He gestured: Mac was to mimic his movements, to mime this bathing, before being taken past more incense to a pitch-black cavern. The man handed him a flashlight, which revealed stories carved into stone, and sleeping bats. Mac felt he should be more interested in these stories but…some riel and a bow released him back into the sunshine, into the warmth of compassionate faces nearly as tall as his entire body.

The disparity in size recreated him as a child, a loved baby. Staring up into a face, the eyes were enormous in their confidence, seeing all of him with only one corner of their gaze. There was tightness in the brow, expressing clarity of vision, wisdom of difficulty. The focus pierced above soft lips.

When he stopped to rest, the faces cradled him in their warm shadows. And when he had recovered his energy, they watched with pride as he jumped from a stone ledge and ducked through a tunnel. Endeared, they smiled as he explored the bas-reliefs. *Apsara* dancers, with beautiful thighs, silently pounded encroaching moss; who will win the ground, the old or the young? *Kala* monsters guarded entryways; what will courage reveal? Green occasionally sprouted from a Bodhisattva forehead, showing recent age, a teasing Hallmark card marking another year. And yet, the smile seemed continuously born anew.

Masterson wandered the grounds, climbing steps, reliving the wonders of a jungle gym, and simultaneously feeling lost in a fun house of benevolent expressions. They were patient for him to fulfill his potential, confident that he would, eventually. He felt their breath in his own lungs, and water came to his eyes. They believed in him.

And he wanted to do them justice.

Returning to the road, Mac sat at one of the two decaying tables, paying for his seat by buying a bottle of water from the woman hovering above a stuffed bucket. He sat to watch the stone faces and to watch other tourists arrive and react. To come out looking wet, kissed, bewildered, new. The other tourists pretended he was not there as they entered Bayon temple—*other tourists are always such an eyesore, aren't they?*—but upon taking their leave, he'd receive a nod. A confused squint into the sun, searching for eye contact. He'd nod back. Y*es, it happened to me too.*

100

Sweat trickled down his neck and he was reminded that he must be careful with time. His watch's wristband had been broken long ago and Mac had decided he liked it better that way. Watches received too much jealous attention in this part of the world, and besides, he felt less anxious, less distracted, when he wasn't constantly aware of the time. Digging through his bag, he found it.

Almost two already! They hadn't even gotten a quarter way through the complex. *How did this happen?* A quick talk with Sree revealed it could take "a little hour," just to finish the circle, so that's what they did, passing only entrances of other temples, Mac promising himself with each painful pass that he would return and see the place properly, perhaps even return many times, perhaps even with Georgia, perhaps even with their kids…

Chapter Eighteen

The car turned onto their street and Mac spotted one of Cate's sons. He was flushed and was kicking a soccer ball up the sidewalk. His brother, a year younger, was trying to steal it and go in the opposite direction. The unevenness and random ice of the sidewalk was sweetening the adrenalin.

I swear they have been playing soccer since they learned to walk. We must still be a couple of hours from dinner. Look how excited they are. Is it Christmas that is depressing me, or was I already depressed? Used to look at humbugs in disbelief; I'd try to toss it up as a recent hardship or a troubled childhood. Now it is those giggles I look at in disbelief.

Christmas as the great segregator between the cheerful and the despondent. Looked up this year and found myself on the wrong side of the line.

From a distance, he saw the back of Inise's daughter; she was busy leading Cate's youngest—*she named him Timothy, right?*—up the stairs. Timmy kept trying to look at his brothers; Samantha obviously wanted to go inside. She had only agreed to coddle this kid to escape the adults. But now the sun was starting to set and she was cold. Scowling, she pulled at Timmy with one hand and blew heat into the mitten of the other. It was the first thing that had made sense to Mac all day.

Chapter Nineteen

Masterson offered to round up Sree's fee to the nearest dollar if he would take him directly to the nearest Internet café. Sree tore his eyes from some tourists consulting a drink peddler, two girls in shorts, and agreed.

The café was expensive. Air-conditioned even. And the attendants were pushing him to "want cold drink." He accepted a curvy glass Coke bottle and dug his watch out of his pocket—2:48. Depending on the Internet speed, checking e-mail could take upward from an hour, or five minutes. *No way to know. But can't be late; unprofessional, disrespectful, shameful even to get caught up in e-mailing one's girlfriend to the point you endanger the drive…*

But there it was. Worth the risk of being late, because there it was already.

She was excited about seeing him. She would be leaving the next day, from LA, having celebrated a decidedly un-holiday dinner with her parents. He could see her facial expressions in her words, as she related her father getting drunk, as usual, and her mother, in her efforts to make-believe sobriety, hitting him, playfully, after every minor infraction. It was a routine they performed even when it was just Georgia in the audience. It usually annoyed her, guessing, probably correctly, that it was a public form of foreplay and, once that was figured out, she could only watch it superimposed with images of Ann and Heath in the throes of awkward passion. But this year, she didn't know, maybe because of Mac's presence in her life, maybe just because she was getting older and saw her parents differently, she found the whole thing kind of sweet. Even the rehearsed goose grope under the garlic cloves, her mother sounding surprised and her father looking innocent, although Georgia could set her watch to it—always, after apps and wine, just as her mother had set oil in a pan—goose! But this time, Georgia had actually laughed instead of turning away in disgust...

The introspection went on, meandering, laced with sweetness, and admitting somewhere that it was late, she was still a bit tipsy from the meal with her parents, and couldn't sleep from excitement. She confirmed again that she had found a connecting flight from Delhi to Phnom Penh, and would be there on the thirtieth. She was tempted to skip the few days they were supposed to have together in India and go straight to Cambodia:

"But the ticket is there, and you've already seen the Taj Mahal anyway...It is too bad you can't come meet me. Hope things are going smoothly for the field project, and that the roads are safe."

Waiting for the reply page to load, Mac felt guilty. *Should I not have gone on this trip to the field? I could have said I already had plans.*

*But they will never stop looking at me like an intern, if I never get any
field experience.*

He drained the last of the soda from the bottle, vacuuming the
bottom rim with the straw. *This is just the way things are going to have
to be sometimes.*

Finally, there was his space, separated from her message with a
line, like a stick at the grocery-store checkout counter. He responded
with understanding of her impatience, describing his tour of Angkor
made a whirlwind just so he would have time to check for her e-mail
before returning to the village. "We have to come back here together."

But he encouraged her not to change her plans. He knew she
wasn't serious about skipping the Taj, but encouraged her anyway to stay
her course, trying to relieve both their guilt over having separate
priorities.

"Agra is hellishly touristy but the Taj Mahal will not disappoint.
Besides, I won't be back in Phnom Penh for a while yet. Looking
forward to celebrating New Year's with you. (You'll celebrate that at
least, won't you?) I will pick you up at the airport. I will be there, but if
something happens and you don't see me, or you are delayed, call the
office. 855-23-210852."

There was a slight distance in the e-mail tone. Or was he just
imagining things? They hadn't seen each other in months. Since those
last days of August. Their e-mails had been a bit syrupy at the beginning.
But then as her trip neared, the tone had dried, perhaps necessarily so,
with all the practical details that needed to be covered: Would he be able
to get off work; the exact days of her January break; when would she
have to return; how much time they would spend in India…Mac was
anxious to show off Cambodia, even if they had originally, during the
summer, planned on meeting in one of his other favorite places, so
maybe they could go from India to Cambodia; would they have enough
106

time; would she have enough time; would rushing through make the visit to one of these countries a waste?

And then the opportunity to go the field had come up for Mac. He would finally be able get some experience in the outer districts, something all the security precautions had thus far made impossible, especially after those three foreigners were kidnapped and killed last year…She had understood, of course, and things had to be rescheduled, with her vacillating whether to try to get a refund for her India ticket. And then it had become obvious that their original plan, for her to leave the States on Christmas Eve, was going to be the cheapest way for her to travel, and since he wasn't going to be done with the project until sometime afterward—exactly when was a point of much annoyance (what if they could have extra days together), as it was impossible to pin down, with security and road conditions being the primary concern—it was decided, she might as well bide her time in India. And it was only a day's trip by bus from Delhi to Agra. So, as much as she would love to see more of the country, maybe she could at least see the famed Taj before leaving…

Mac thought maybe he detected fear; somehow arriving in India alone didn't seem as scary as arriving in Cambodia alone. But Mac wanted to be in Phnom Penh to greet her anyway. He wanted to be responsible for her first impressions of the country he was falling for, so he thought it an excellent plan, and tried to relieve her guilt for not spending more time with her parents before leaving, and for wanting to still do part of the vacation they had planned as a twosome, by herself.

All this, in the last few months, had dominated the e-mails, which were fairly regular, every other day, until Mac left Phnom Penh with the medics to cover an outlying province. That interruption had given doubts room to flourish in the fertility of an isolated mind.

Is the professor that she keeps mentioning hitting on her? Where are they having these deep conversations about broaching difficult topics in the classroom? Where exactly is teaching sex ed being discussed? In the lecture room, hallway, over dinner...Perhaps she is becoming so involved with the Harlem tutoring project, that she is deciding she can better work in the United States? She does nothing but rave about her students. Is she feeling a "sense of calling" among the inner city school system...Does she still dream of me?

When her delicious gushing started to be replaced by fibrous fact, he hadn't been able to continue spooning cream out himself, just to see if it would be returned. It had felt too great a risk. He didn't want to be the sappy one. He wanted to be strong, practical, someone she could count on, someone who she could plan things with easily, without whining about desperately wanting to see her, wanting to kiss her, touch her, smell her, lick her, caress her, listen to her...So Mac had tried to follow her lead, and was only as sweet as she was to him, and so it had ebbed recently...

But isn't planning to meet up for one's vacation, isn't the planning and the working out the particulars, pretty romantic in itself? Or has a distance really grown, and am I just being stupid, feeling like everything should be exactly the same as I left it, not realizing she has kept moving forward in her own life there, without me? Is this long-distance longing just too much of a strain? There are surely plenty of opportunities for her to be with other men...

Or is this just my paranoia? A paranoia she will laugh at when she arrives. She said she was looking forward to seeing me. But perhaps her heart has grown conflicted. Perhaps she isn't as sure as she was before I left. Perhaps part of the reason she is looking forward to seeing me is so she can relieve some of that conflict, decide if she was right this summer when she made all those promises, was correct in her feelings for me, or if absence has just made it all fade away...

It doesn't matter; she is coming. At least, it sounds like she has decided to come. When we see each other, all the doubts will disappear. I am sure. We will get through this year. Won't we?

Mac's stomach garbled up acidic against the carbonation—3:10. He decided not to check any other e-mails. He had to eat or he would be a grouch on the drive back. He rose into vertigo and realized he hadn't eaten anything since the coffee and rice porridge at breakfast. Feeling faint and impatient at the entrance, he called out, trying to get the attention of someone in the back. The TV was on; a soccer video game was being worshipped by a crowd of boys. But finally, one kid hit another kid in the arm and motioned to Mac. After one more long look at the game, he ran over to the desk. After Mac tried to peer over to the set while simultaneously, and thus clumsily, working on the lock of a metal box, the boy eventually handed him some change.

Mac escaped the close quarters only to be engulfed in heat. The sidewalk was made of intermittent slabs of concrete over a high gutter. Navigating the deep holes and the aggressive peddlers, he somehow made it the five blocks to the spot he was to meet the driver—360-degree turn. Tourist restaurants abounded, catering to dehydrated Angkor visitors, most of whom were UN workers on holiday. The restaurants, with names cueing off the temples themselves, offered a range of local and western food. The misspellings were endearing. There was Fired Potato and Stemed Veg. And a place boasting "Typical Food." The latter's wipe board promised Eggs with Toasts, Big Mac served Fried, and their specialty, the Typical Sandwitch served with Cold Slow. Most of these open-air cafes were completely empty, except the one advertising a daylong happy hour bedecked by local dance.

The Maharaja Restaurant sat kitty-corner from their meeting place. Some quick Indian food just might be the ticket. They looked like they might even have air conditioning.

Georgia's probably eatin' Indian—3:32. Service will probably be slow. But maybe there's enough time.

He settled into a too small chair, under a flower-patterned table bedecked ridiculously with another flower, a fake in a small vase. A young boy handed him a menu, and then ran away when Mac tried to order. An older man came out. A ready smile surrounded by dark heavy skin.

"Hello, sir, what can I do to help you today?"

"Well, I would like to order some food."

"Certainly sir; what would you like?"

"I would like your tomato-*panir uttapan*."

"Uh sorry, sir, we are out."

"OK, how 'bout the panir *dosa*?"

"No, no."

"*Masala* dosa?"

"I am sorry, sir."

"What do you have?"

"I think plain dosa, sir."

"Sounds good," he concluded, handing back the worthless menu.

The man continued to stand there.

"I'll have one of those."

"Which sir?"

"The plain dosa!"

Nods were exchanged and the man shouted into the kitchen. A woman's voice shouted back and the man excused himself to investigate.

Mac sighed. The boy slipped him a bowl of water. Mac hungrily eyed the lime floating in it as the couple discussed the order. Restraining himself from actually sucking on the fruit, feeling the boy's eyes on his neck from the corner, Mac dipped his fingers in the bowl. He checked that he could see the street from his seat.

But he was in luck. Once the debate was finished, dosas were one of the quickest things to prepare. It arrived on a wide platter, a stiff roll of crepe, rice and lentil flour flash-fried, and surrounded by assorted splatters and cups of sauces. There was lentil soup, red-onion chutney, coconut chutney, green mint sauce, black tamarind. The range of colors created an artist's palette and the dosa was his paintbrush dipping among the flavors. Cleaning the platter, he quickly created a satisfied stomach, preceded only by savory tongue.

The man came out, smiling at how fast the meal had disappeared. "Would you like anything else? Some chai maybe?"

Now 3:58. "Umm, no, just the check, please."

"Bill?"

"Bill." Mac stood corrected.

Paying, stalling, dreading the heat, *where's the driver?*

"Where are you from?" the owner started.

"The United States. America. Yourself?"

"Bombay, but I grew up in South Thailand, and I have been here for thirty years."

Through the window they both watched his kid and wife walk out from the back of the restaurant. They had identical postures, sliding around in flip-flops. She was a round woman, under a bamboo hat, dragging her child with a hand that was several shades lighter than her son's forearm. Her own forearm hooked through a basket, presumably off for some shopping, trying to escape eye-contact with both customer and husband.

111

"Where's your wife from?"

"A village a day that way," gesturing vaguely and pulling out a chair to join Mac. Mac squelched his agitation. The owner sat with exhaustion and fingered the peeling lamination on the table. Turning again to the figures disappearing in the window, talking more to them than to Mac, he continued, "My parents wanted to arrange a marriage for me; they wanted me to have good Indian children. But I convinced them I was in love over here, such a pretty girl, such light skin and so young. I told them how the gods were showing their favor; I already did business with her parents. They had a chicken farm back then and I worked for them when...when I needed to."

Hoping to lighten the mood, Mac teased him about now having a vegetarian restaurant, putting his in-laws out of business after stealing their daughter. The owner suddenly looked hungry, "We would've been *non-veg* if the eggs hadn't gone soft; you should try my butter chicken..."

"Whad'ya mean 'the eggs went soft'?"

"Right after my son was born, the egg shells went soft. Her parents think the chickens were cursed. Even if sometimes a chick was able to hatch from those shells, they were afraid of it."

"Yeah, I can see that."

"So now they live here," he waved his hand at the ceiling, indicating the apartment above. "Her brother is still on the farm, trying to find a better chicken. The chicken's first eggs are always good, but before long the curse gets them too, and the search starts again. I try to send him money but..."

"And your parents?"

"My parents said they warned me. Their restaurant in Thailand was non-veg too; they were afraid of the curse. So even though they

112

always said they love their grandson, they died without ever seeing him. Now my wife's parents are my only parents."

"It is good of you to take care of your wife's parents."

Shrugging, he said, "It's my job. Sometimes they even remind me of my parents, except," smiling, "they don't like my cooking very much. But my wife knows how to make rice for them, and rice for me. And my son will eat it all…"

"Still it can't be easy, all of you living together?" Mac finally recognized his role as concerned listener, a role with which he was familiar: He has the blank wide face perfect for the job. Solo travelers, transient and lonely, were often met with the same confessionals that inundate taxi drivers and bartenders. Mac coaxed the overripe words from the man, gobbling them up himself, now genuinely interested and hoping to hear it all before he had to leave.

"Her mother helps grind the curry; she is getting blind, and it makes her sneeze, and makes her knuckles hurt, but she still likes to help. But her father is sad, or maybe mad. I don't know. He complains a lot."

"What does he complain about?"

"Well, like, it is hard for them to unfold all the way at nighttime. Their bodies, especially Grandmother's, are used to being bent—working rice paddies and chasing after chickens. And they have lots of nightmares, you know?"

Mac nodded recognition, but didn't interrupt. Most of the population had nightmares dating from the reign of the Khmer Rouge.

"They whimper as they try to sleep. I tried to get them a bed. I thought it might be softer and help them sleep better. But they were afraid of the height, and felt unsafe in the softness. They prefer the floor. So I sleep on that bed and try not to wake them when my feet hit the ground near their heads in the morning.

"The roosters wake my son and me up every day, even here in the city, but somehow my wife and her parents sleep right through it. I think they block it out. After spending so much time waiting for eggs to form properly, they are deaf with anger at the entire animal—chicken or rooster. They feel betrayed.

"Sometime I think it is ironic," he used the word proudly, "that her parents seem to be made of nothing but hard shell, unable to unfold, crumbling slowly, slowly, and yet their chickens, after my son was born, would only produce unprotected babies." Pausing as if the timing unnerved him, as if he was wondering if his dark skin was to blame.

Mac saw the jeep pass the window and slow. It stopped diagonally from the restaurant—4:29. "Well, it sounds like you are doing everything you can to make things easier on them."

"Yeah, the restaurant is a good business; even when we are doing badly one month, we can eat the food that we were hoping to sell to customers. And it is not bad food, eh?" he said, grinning, remembering the way Mac had wolfed it all down.

"The food was delicious!"

"The Indians like it when they come. But we don't get a lot of Frenchies like you."

"Well, it's not the food's fault. I've gotta go. That's my ride."

"Tell your friends to come, OK?"

"Sure!"

As Mac approached, the driver took a last drag from a cigarette. He had the pack prominently displayed, boasting an American brand, on the hood as he pretended not to watch the girls running a *satay* stand.

The air conditioning in the jeep had been going full blast. It wafted up against Mac's chest as he got in. The clock on the dashboards told him that 4:35 is close enough to 4:00 p.m. He checked his ingrained
114

punctuality. His mouth was parched and his eyes a bit droopy. *Should have gotten that chai.*

As they drove, the few tourist awnings of English dropped away and were replaced by huts of dry groceries. Often, these stands were abutted by a wood table of men, busy gambling and drinking *arak* out of recycled bottles. A woman and toddler sat in a doorway. She pointed out the jeep to the fussing kid and tried to force him to wave.

Why doesn't he have a happy hour, like many of the restaurants around there? Perhaps he is Muslim? His parents left Bombay for Southern Thailand. Maybe.

Mac's thoughts boomeranged through the day and, outside his window, an hour passed. Women and men were still hooked like canes in the rice paddies as the light dimmed. Their conical hats became silhouetted against the sky. A man, putting a finishing tie on a bamboo fence, was close enough to the road to make brief eye contact with Mac.

Perhaps they are washing the eggs with a disinfectant, he came full circle. *A common mistake. But he described the shells as soft, not brittle. Just inadequate English?*

The driver stopped to allow a herd of water buffalo file through. A grass whip swung amid a boy's "hzzt's" and "ya!s." A younger boy followed, using a long reed to imitate his brother, but with doubled enthusiasm. The driver unrolled his window and asked about the ferry.

A calcium deficiency, perhaps? Could be something downstream of calcium in the shell formation, but calcium would be a good starting spot...I imagine the timing of the calcium supplement would have to be exact...What would the best source be?

Two hours later, they arrived at the ferry crossing. A small yellow dress, caked with dirt, ran, yelling importantly to the man who had just finished docking his ferry. He had already looked up at the headlights. A whiff of boiled rice came from a thatched roof, as the child was called away. The driver and the ferry operator bargained.

"He wants us to pay double. He says it is going to rain. It will be his last run for the night."

"Fine."

The jeep was loaded, driving over two perfectly placed planks. Under the ferry, the river was an invisible gloss. The child's whine against a bath was more salient than the water.

Once on the other side, the village was only an hour away. They had made remarkable time. But Mac had hardly noticed. His mind was excitedly rotating through all the angles of shell production.

A few drops of water fell prematurely on the windshield, as their headlights illuminated hammock homes in huts he could see through. Sheets hung as walls and mud lay where tile should be. Mac remembered a line from a poem Georgia wrote: The rain falls on us all the same.

As they approached, Mac could make out Kacham collecting hung-dry laundry. The man waved into the headlights. Behind him, lightning cracked hard through a soft sky.

Chapter Twenty

While waiting for change from the taxi driver, he watched Inise's daughter fold Timothy's little leg up the doorway's step. The girl was greeted by her mother, who asked her a question. But instead of listening to the response, Inise's attention was captured by Mac coming up the stairs. She exited the house, no coat, and a stiff slosh of gin in a mug. She closed the door behind her.

"Want some?"

"Desperately." Mac dropped the duffel bag on the porch. It clanged, to his surprise. *Oh yeah, the arak bottle.*

"So," Inise welcomed as Mac gulped, "there's more people than usual."

"Really? I thought Mom wanted to keep things calm for Dad."

"I think she is trying to hide Dad from herself."

"That bad, huh?"

"He's not the same, Mac."

"Of course not. Did Gram make it here?"

"Yeah, she got here today, and as soon as Cate's kids came back from sledding, she went up for a nap. She has already made it obvious she misses her nursing home. They pick her up tomorrow. She recognizes Dad even less than we do. Mac, she sleeps in the black pearls Gramps gave to her..." Inise teetered a bit.

Mac looked her over. "Maybe you should give me some more of that."

"Sure," she said, handing back the mug. "Samantha asked if she could go to Slade's for Christmas this year."

"Oh, man."

"Yeah."

The door opened. "Greg—" Cate appeared with her youngest on her hip; he was playing with her collar and the flat gold chain around her neck. "Oh, sorry, I thought—oh, Mac, you are here too. I am so glad you could make it this year."

"I make it every year, Cate."

"I know. But it's from so far; it always seems surprising that you show up. Anyway, sorry, Inise, have you seen Greg? I am about to get urine soaked all the way though my blouse and it's his turn to change the diaper."

"Yeah, he has been capitalized by Lyle in the back. Go save him before Greg has signed the hospital over to him."

Cate missed the joke. "But Greg just handles the insurance paperwork. He doesn't have any authority. He just does what he is told."

Her last statement made Mac snort. But Inise stayed the course, "Well, don't tell premed that or Mom will have an empty place setting."

Cate was still blinking at Mac's snort. "At least *Greg* is helping his family."

118

"I didn't mean—" Mac started, but Cate had swiveled on her heel, back into the house.

"Don't mind her. She thought Dad was gonna be her fallback man for the rest of her life. This stroke has shaken us all out of a bit of a dream, I think. The last few months haven't been easy, Mac."

He nodded, handed back her mug, and looked at his bag. It suddenly seemed pathetically empty.

"Anyway," she continued, "we should go in. She'll tell everyone you are here."

Chapter Twenty-One

In oily darkness, they stood next to a swell of river, getting just enough breeze to remind them night was passing. The lights at the ends of three cigarettes were the main festivity. They touched to form an orange orb and released a Christmas cheer for Mac's sake.

"…and let there be many more holidays to come," Kacham exhaled. The couple's eyes hooked together, while Mac swallowed the dregs of an Angkor Beer. The bottle still sported the semblance of a celebratory bow fashioned from a plastic bag, a present from Kacham and Radath.

Kacham leaned into Radath's ear in a rare moment of public intimacy. Mac looked down, and then out, politely pretending he could make out the water and wondering how to make an exit.

Kacham unlinked and said, "See how high the water is? It is the wrong season to have so much rain."

120

But Mac wanted a storm; he hoped it drowned out the sound of them having an erotic holiday.

"Well, shower, or no shower, I am gonna go bathe." They didn't catch his pun. He quickly continued, "Good night, you two. Thanks for the beer. And Merry Christmas."

He hurried off to the far corner, passing the caretaker's sleeping house. There was some dense shrubbery, which he used to hang up his shirt and pants. The toilet holes were to the right and the water pump to the left. Standing in his boxers, he located the flashlight hung on a rope from the shrubs.

A bucket was waiting under the pump, steadied by a bamboo mat that was losing its battle against mud and slime. While filling the bucket, he realized he had forgotten his soap in his room. He would have to risk interrupting the doctors if he went back to fetch it now. Behind the bucket, an unbelievably white Asian woman advertised detergent from a bag caked with dirt. Soap is soap, whether marketed for laundry or body. He hoped the chief's wife wouldn't mind his theft.

He and the medics were lucky to have this temporary living arrangement. It was a little more comfortable than their last home stay. The village chief had somehow retained an extra building, perhaps an out-of-use barn and chicken coop, which had been easily converted to provide two bedrooms. And the chief's wife made sure to serve them a generous helping of soup and rice at every meal.

He palmed water over his body, scrubbed powdered soap soft, and battled suds with the bucket. When he finished, he returned everything—flashlight, detergent, and shrubbery—to their original positions. Swishing in wet boxers, he ran on tiptoe through the dirt, clothes and shoes dampening in a bundle against his chest. A wooden tray of incense and jasmine garlands, a spirit house, looked eerily transient in the lightning. Awkwardly, he climbed the ladder to their

121

rooms, trying to scrape the bottoms of his feet clean on the first step. He found his towel and wrapped it around his hips. From underneath, he inched the boxers off with curious modesty. The medics had gone to bed and he was alone.

It had been a long day, but flashes of light charged the air with adrenalin, drawing Mac back out to the overhang. He leaned from the railing into the sleek black sky. Every three seconds, light flooded clouds, huts, trees, endless rice paddies, with white silver. It felt like the world was ending. He imagined it was not lightning, but guerilla warfare. In reality, a remaining stronghold of the insurgency was not that far off. *That's the direction, right?* He had heard that even government soldiers didn't dare cross the provincial border.

The last wires of electricity gave up. The winds dipped their temperatures and finally painted the storm tangible. Oozing rain. A door slammed. A flashlight appeared in the neighboring hut, a candle, and then nothing. Silver everything, and then we all disappear.

He moved to his room, to lie upon the hard mattress. Little particles of dirt stuck to his already sweating back. She was coming in less than a week. *This storm better not make the ferry crossings impossible. The roads can't get much worse, can they?*

Heaven spit through the screen to splatter upon his face. He listened to the approaching storm, and let it guide the rhythm of his hand in his crotch. He saw her, Georgia, and Radath—her soft and blond, she maroon and sharp. They helped him stroke by making each other happy. Tongues. Too pink and wet. Curling around each other. And then Georgia's tongue following Radath's strong jaw to her ear, to the back of her neck. Radath took over, tracing Georgia's trachea, lingering at the soft pit intersection of her collarbone, and then jumping to an erect breast. Georgia arched her back in pleasure, and suddenly Radath was replaced by Mac. He saw the nipple up close, little hairs and follicles

122

tightening in mauve, before the swell of flesh. Flipping, tearing the sheet aside, Georgia found her own hold. She took the stem into her mouth, hiding her breasts, but, over her shoulder, she revealed ripe curves of buttocks. And then, in his mind's eye, there were only butt curves, dozens of them, undersides, top sides, profiles, cracks, cleavage, standing, lying, sitting, pulsing in his lap...

He was about to add his own white streak to the blackness when the shutters at his window violently clapped their own thunder. The sky's stomach was suddenly slit wide open. Its contents gushed down. *How can it be this full?* But then he did come after all, and he drowned in sleep, still fondling himself, or rather dreaming of Georgia fondling him, and telling her with creased forehead how worried he was about how the huts he saw today would look tomorrow.

Chapter Twenty-Two

Entering the house, after forty-five hours of traveling, he was smelly. The sticky residue of the soap in the Tokyo transfer hotel had long been replaced by sweat. His shirt had been made crisp for a moment in the cold, but the freezing air did nothing to kill the bacteria growing under his armpits. His entire being begged for a shower. But first he had to get through the reception.

Stinky hugs for all; I'm back. Yep, gone totally native, your son, your brother, your relative. At least you don't have to deal with me as much as I do.

He followed the whiff of gin from Inise's mug into the hallway. There wasn't much of a foyer, just three choices for movement once the door closed behind him. To the right, an ajar door hid a living area, which fanned into the rest of the first floor. Or he could go straight, past the radiator, into the sterile kitchen, shellacked against the rest of the house, emphasis put on easy cleanup. To the left, stairs emptied from the

124

second-floor bedrooms directly to the outside door; they were a teenager's dream. It was those stairs, which he had escaped up and down so many times before, that beckoned him now. But first, his arrival was sure to gather attention.

He could hear Cate's voice coming from the back study. There were several walls between him and her words, but from her tone, Mac guessed that sarcasm was being used to quietly argue with her husband in the presence of their cousin. But other than this remote scene, his aromatic entry was received with silence.

Peeking through the living room door, Inise noticed her daughter. The girl was profiled in a hooking posture, curled toward the thick book on her lap.

"Samantha, have you said hello to your uncle?"

"Hi." She didn't look up. She had already peeked at whom her mother was talking to, through the window. A palm came up and waved toward the door.

"Hi there. What'ya reading?" Mac tried.

Without taking her eyes from the page, she turned the book so Mac could see the cover. It was bound like an old library volume. Stamped in the stubborn surface the title read, *The Brothers Grimm in Archetype and Allegory.*

"Wow."

Inise nodded, her face in a tug of war between a smile and a frown. "She found it on my shelf. I had forgotten all about it, until she started carrying it around with her. She studies the pictures like gospel."

Samantha pretended not to hear her mother. A kettle sounded. An uneasy shuffle hurried on the floor above and then slowed. Mac looked up to see his mother navigating the first few stairs. She saw Mac through the railing, "Oh, you are here! Already. Everyone is here already. I haven't even finished getting my makeup on."

"Oh you don't need makeup for me, Mom."

"Yes, but your cousin is here too, and…That kettle is atrocious; I am so sorry."

"I got it, Mom." Inise slowly read the hint.

"Oh, Mac, I am so glad to see you," his mother told the stair. She watched each foot take its place on a new platform. Mac, annoyed, wondered if she was acting older than she was. *Did Dad's stroke make her think they are both ten years older?* She got to the bottom and looked up at Mac. *Was she always this short?*

"Look at you. Such a big man you've become. I feel stronger just knowing you are here."

One hug and it all felt like it did last year. Only perhaps his mother was a little lighter as he picked her up.

She squealed. "I am too old for that now," she added with laughter.

Her hair smelled of dryer heat and hair spray. *All the messy parts of dinner must be already done.* Setting her down, he planted a kiss on a cheek of perfumed rouge. But he did so too rote-ly.

"What's wrong?"

"Nothing, Mom," he said, looking down at his bag. "Do you mind if I take a shower? I feel rather scummy."

"Sure, honey, but I need to get a final handle on how many seats to set. Is your girlfriend here too?" she asked, searching his eyes, rather than the hallway.

Mac looked at her, astounded, "No, Mom. I told you that."

"Right. Sorry, just wanted to make sure. Anyway it is good to have a man in the house."

"What about Dad?"

"Yes, you should at least go say hi to him before you shower. Oh, it was his tea that I was making."

126

Mute, he followed his mother into the kitchen where Inise already had a tea bag in place. She was reaching into the cabinet.

"Inise! Don't give him a saucer! We aren't gonna have enough bread plates as it is." Digressing into a bitter mumble, his mother turned her attention to the stove. "We had a matching set of twelve when we first got married…"

"If I don't get a separate bread plate, I'm leaving," Mac tried.

They both ignored him. "But what's Dad gonna do with his tea bag?"

"Give him a napkin or something. At least he can't break that."

Inise turned her glare from her mother back to the cabinet. Her hand moved down a shelf and grabbed another mug from the plethora of souvenir and joke gifts. Without another word, she left the kitchen, trailing an empty mug in one hand while the other wrist guided the tea.

Mac saw her gin mug, now empty, on the counter. *Where can I get me some of that?*

His mother moved to the sink and started counting the water glasses, wine glasses, dinner plates, stacked overhead. Exactly the kind of attention Mac wanted. He grabbed a coffee mug from the shelf his sister had just left and opened the liquor cabinet underneath the counter. The gin his sister was drinking was in the forefront. He filled the coffee mug halfway.

"Mac, before you see your father, can you reach up and see if there is a plate…"

This was the kind of blindness he appreciated. No observation that there wasn't ice in his gin, nor tonic, and, yes, the glass was that full of alcohol alone.

Unsuccessful with finding a lost plate on the upper shelf, Mac moved on from the kitchen. In the next room, Inise clutched the dining

127

room table, leaning into it, as if she couldn't decide whether she was using it to hold her up or hold her back. She looked at her feet. A bowl of grapes sat in front of her, flanked by a cutting board of cheese and crackers and a baby cup of cashews. Mac approached with his mug. He reached into her line of vision and grabbed a grape. When Inise didn't look up, he pushed the seedless gray against the roof of his mouth, sucked the dry flesh and waited.

"Want some?" he tried, lifting his mug.

Taking the mug, Inise met Mac's eyes and then stared in the direction of the kitchen. "The man likes a saucer; he should have one."

"Ah, she's just afraid there aren't gonna be enough plates for all of us."

"No, she's afraid there isn't gonna be enough husband for herself." Inise's eyes, lined in red, remained open over the rim of the coffee cup.

Mac looked down at a cracker. He pushed it into the Brie. It broke in the cheese. He tossed the top half in his mouth while concentrating on rescuing the other half and securing the portioned wedge of smushed Brie. The cheese smeared into his mouth, masking the cracker and mixing into a sour sponge his tongue couldn't negotiate. It used to be Dad who made Mom tea at the end of the day.

Chapter Twenty-Three

"Thanks for agreeing to drive on your day off."

"No problem; I happy to meet your wife," Haing voiced sincerely.

Mac laughed and corrected him. 'Girlfriend' was such a foreign concept.

"I am sorry, sir."

"Doesn't matter." Mac was smiling into the windshield, almost giddy with anticipation.

The dust on Phnom Penh looked lit from beneath as Mac tried to see it from Georgia's eyes. She was going to find the dirt and decay endearing, he was sure. She'd comment on the juxtaposition of French architecture in a tropical climate. She would swing from happy to heartbroken and back again, as he took her from temples to cardboard slums, from Tuol Sleng to the river promenade. And finally, a trip to Angkor was planned for right before her departure.

She would want to try every dish, and they would share cheap French wine, and celebrate New Year's, as they talked about how it would be after she graduated—when she could come and stay—how they would do these sorts of things all the time...*Perhaps I should suggest she take some French? Is that imposing?*

But in all their talk of exploring, the bedroom would be where they tasted every part, and she, downy and fragrant, would lie in his arms, smiling contentedly into the darkness, with no concern for daybreak. *God, I can't wait to taste her. Smell her. Touch her.* He was so excited he could hardly endure it. *One more hour.*

"Can we stop up ahead, so I can check my e-mail? Make sure her plane isn't delayed?"

He sallied into the little room stuffed with laughably small cubicles. He had to worm through sideways to get to number eight. His butt ached its way to the tiny hard stool, reminding him of yesterday's long and bouncy trip back to Phnom Penh in the medics' jeep. He was already looking forward to the day when he wouldn't feel obligated to take the backseat.

The keyboard had dust between the keys, and some were yellow with use. He sat in front of the plastic box, waiting for the connection to be established, feeling a bit too big for the stool he was balanced upon. Finally. This place even had a little clock ticking in the corner. Hi-tech. Log-in, the oh-so-secret password, *would I tell Georgia it if she asked,* and a full six minutes later, he arrived at an inbox. It was even *his* inbox. Two messages.

The one from Georgia, apeachaday@columbia.edu, dated the twenty-seventh, read: *Masterson, just got to Agra. You were right. This place is awful, but I am going to take your advice and stay the night so I can see the Taj at sunrise. Shouldn't be too hard. I am awfully jet-lagged still. I am sure to be asleep within the hour. Sorry this is so short. I have so much to say, so much I want to talk to you about...but I am afraid of losing the connection. I really need to talk to you. I'll try again tomorrow. Georgia.*

The second one, with the next day's date, was from her father's e-mail address. Mac had been unreachable by phone for weeks, while they were traveling the outer provinces; perhaps her father carried a message from her? A plane delay? Or, more probably, it was also from her. She often used the family account when the pine system was being problematic. It took an eternity to load.

Twenty minutes were logged staring blankly at the backlit message. And then Mac got up and caught the stool as it took a precarious angle. His mouth traced sick smiles he couldn't control. Forgetting to sign out, he ebbed his way through the aisle, on tiptoe, facing the other wall this time. He hadn't noticed the puppy and house posters before. A sixteen-by-twenty-inch picture of a potted plant. He had to turn 180 degrees in order to face the owner and pay. He watched his hand tremble at his wallet.

Grinning, almost laughing, a tug of war between his mouth and the crease of his brow, Mac got in next to Haing. Nauseated, *at least now I don't have to sit in the back with her stuff.* They drove a decade of minutes, until Mac realized the driver's knowledge was still stuck in the past.

"Please drop me at Tuol Sleng. And don't wait for me. I'll take a taxi back."

The driver's arms grew stiff. Their alarm was annoying.

"But, sir, what about—"

"Please! Go to Tuol Sleng!"

Silence.

131

A bland former high school appeared, surrounded by lines and loops of barbed wire. It had been used as the main "interrogation" center of the Khmer Rouge.

Climbing out of the jeep, Mac said, "Thank you, Haing."

"You can call me if you need to go to the airport later, sir."

Mac nodded, swallowed the acid in his throat, and slammed the door.

Holding his breath, he paid his two dollars and strode hastily by manicured trees and an overgrown lawn. He had been there before, and he walked with speed and confidence toward his destination. He exhaled violently as he passed the large board that explained the former torture center's "Rules": you were not to question any order, nor pretend you were not a traitor to the revolution. Punishment for disobedience or doubt was certain; ten lashes were equal to five electrical shocks.

Rooms of shackles gave way to rooms of pictures. Hundreds and hundreds of faces, each with a different stare. And a different number. Mac paused, reeling, in front of a board of mostly children. A boy stared defiantly into the camera, with confusion only a layer behind. Disbelief and shock dripped down his eyebrows. He looked about eight.

That's how old I was when this was happening.

The boy's ears stuck out, protruding enough to be teased—Mac's only childhood torture. The child's turtleneck offered no protection from the number that had been safety-pinned to his chest. No protection from being renamed number 5.

Perhaps if he had been arrested later, the boy would have been selected, trained, mutated into a prison guard. Like hundreds of other preteens, slowly finding pleasure in exceptional cruelty.

What would have happened to me? Would I have been selected? How proud I would have been...

But Mac stopped thinking. The horror was too salient.

132

He exited the bare classrooms to the courtyard. Chin-up bars stood naked, stripped of their use as gallows and interrogation spots. Around to another building, Mac paused only briefly at the makeshift brick prison cells that lined the bottom-floor classrooms. He wanted to go higher. He climbed the stairs, imagining looking up the skirts of uniformed high school girls. Someone had graffitied algebra on the wall. Fractions. Divisors.

Upstairs, dark wood partitioned a classroom into sixteen cells. How lucky to get your own cell, instead of shackled *en mass* to a common pole at your foot. Mac entered number seven from the aisle. There was an old metal box, strewn on the ground. It was clean now of the excrement it must have contained; cell inhabitants had requested permission from the guards, of course, before defiling it. The door had a slide metal lock on the outside, far below a single opening, a hole the width of a hand. On the other side of this body-length cell, a proper classroom window held an old-fashioned shutter along with its bars. From inside the cell, Mac imagined kids flirting on the balcony. Their laughter morphed into shrieks of electrocution.

He turned to face the wall. He appreciated the close quarters. He stood like that, not moving, face tilted down, inches from the wall, just staring at the closeness of the wood. And only at the wood. Focusing on a single grain.

After each age of cold minutes, his eyes blurred the pattern. He'd blink and regain his focus. Determined to consume the grain's texture, oil, history. Wishing it would consume him instead.

He stood like that, not moving, with hands pressed against his thighs to keep his stance steady. For an incalculable time. Until too many tourists had given him the once-over. Until he thought he might vomit.

He exited through the cell door and followed the guard's aisle to the balcony. He clasped the barbed wire, put up to prevent untimely suicide. He felt nothing. He tightened his grip. It broke the skin. He blubbered for the slightest moment and held on tight, hating himself for even having a passing thought about infection.

In the courtyard, a child at a run, in flip-flops and flowing pants, stopped to fix her hair in the wind. She kicked at the palm leaves in the dirt, aware her rush was just for fun, and then continued on through the gate into the neighborhood.

Seventeen thousand passed through the prison/reeducation center, all meticulously biographied, measured, and photographed; seven survived. Mac left without paying his respects to the piles of skulls.

Chapter Twenty-Four

"How would I say it in Khmer?" Mac fondled Ria's breast. They were both a little filmy from the night of sex, but the morning light had made it all seem new again. Mac was energetic with a curiosity he hadn't felt in years.

"Khmer is so boring. Say it in French." Ria was lying on his bed, thin and bare. Her breath was fresh with the toothpaste she had snuck out to swallow before he awoke. Her hair was gently brushed. It was their fourth weekend together and she had a sense of routine.

"I don't know French."

"You don't know Khmer either," she teased, dotting his nose with her finger.

"But I am trying to learn." He kissed her nipple, "Come on; how would I say 'nipple' in Khmer?"

Ria blushed, "Why do you always want to learn Khmer?"

Bouncing between breasts atop the delicateness of her chest bone, alternating words with kisses, he explained "The. Better. To. Seduce. You. With. My. Dear."

Ria wiggled out from underneath him and sat on the edge of the bed. Her feet dangled a bit off the floor. Into the concave of her belly, she whispered, "French is better."

He kissed her protruding spine. She pretended not to notice and stood up. She gathered last night's clothes off the floor and placed them on the seat of a chair. Sorting, she folded his onto the back of the chair and untangled hers to put back on.

Mac came up behind her and stooped to pass his lips along her neck. He rested his chin on her shoulder. "You know, the French would stay naked and have breakfast in bed."

She froze for a moment, and he took the opportunity to start sucking on the small pointy bones at her shoulder. He ran his hands down the back of her arms to wrap around her wrists. Her body relaxed a bit and her neck opened with an invitation.

"In fact, the French would probably go back to bed before even considering breakfast."

She smiled as he kissed the length of her jawbone. That smile was all the permission he needed. He scooped her up and plopped her back onto the bed.

Landing with a bounce, she laughed, "What else would the French do?"

"Ravage each other senseless!" He buried his head in her stomach and shook it as vigorously as a dog. She screamed, thrashing with giggles. He reached up to hold down her arms, while he moved on to rub his face against the sides of her pelvis. His tongue pulled at her hipbones, forcefully, until her laughter dissipated into a sigh.

He tried to go farther down, but she squirmed down with him, trying to reposition them, so that she could pleasure him instead. He came up to her ear, pushing his hard member against her outer thigh. He whispered, "A French woman would let me keep exploring."

She suddenly became very still, waiting. At her side, Mac moved both her wrists into his left hand and brought his right hand to her knee. She breathed. He massaged up her thigh, pulsing the leg against himself, "Do you like that?

She nodded, and then bit her lower lip as he placed his hand directly atop her small mound of hair. He undulated his hand against the folds and rubbed himself into her leg. He pushed harder as her breath slowed to follow his rhythm. But when he inserted his finger to find her pearl of excitement hard and ready, she gasped. She gulped while he gently, quickly, moved it up and down. The vibration echoed across her pelvis into his. She tried to grab for him but he held her wrists tightly. He licked his middle finger and started the vibration again. "Do you like that?" he whispered.

She smiled and buried her head into his neck. Her shoulders were tense. But the rest of her body surrendered. His collarbone was rising with deep breaths as she began gasping into his chest. Dry-humping her side, into her soft thigh and buttocks, and vibrating her clit, faster, faster, everything became moist, as she thrashed her head and arms, trying not to scream, biting him as she came with a gushing cry.

Out of breath and in tingly confusion, she took advantage of the new slack at her wrists to turn to her side and hide her face completely in his chest hair. The bed was still vibrating; she thought it was she that was still vibrating, but when she peeked out, she saw Mac's hand finishing the strokes that caused him to soil his stomach and sheets.

He expelled a surplus of air and was newly bathed in sweat. She was lying very still, hands pressed together between her thighs. He moved his hand to her back. There seemed to still be a slight quiver in her rib cage. Their breath normalized and she looked up from his chest to check his eyes for her evaluation.

"Did you like that?" he asked.

She blushed with a wide smile, nodded, and buried her head back into his chest, trying not to notice the tiny teeth marks she left there.

Chapter Twenty-Five

Greg entered the dining room from the back study, carrying his toddler and trailed by his wife. "Oh, Mac, good to see you, man. I'd shake your hand but apparently I have some diaper changing to do."

"You won't find me arguing with you there."

The boy twisted with a broken whine.

"I won't argue with him either."

"Can't blame him myself," Greg concurred, shooting a look at his wife. "I'll be right back."

Fingering another seedless grape, Mac asked his sister, "So did you guys stay here again this year?"

"Ya, it's just easier than getting a hotel. Especially with the kids."

"Uh huh."

"Why are you smirking?"

"No reason. Where's Lyle?"

"Talking to Dad."

Pause. Inise drank Mac's gin. Putting her hands on her hips, trying to think of something to say, Cate watched Mac load another cracker. Mac piled it especially high, knowing his sister was morally against cholesterol. "So I heard you flew into New York City. Why not just fly directly here?"

"Had some errands to do there," he lied, paying extraordinary attention to the powdered rind of the Brie. "But didn't get them done; the plane was delayed."

"How was the security?"

"Why do you always ask that?" Inise exhaled, releasing a stench of gin.

Her siblings paid her no attention. "You know, the plane was standard, but there were new rules at Port Authority. They needed my address."

"That's smart. Any foreigners are gonna come through New York first. They really need to crack down on this before something major happens. You know we had a bomb threat in Springfield this year; supposedly he came through New York."

"So," Mac started, chewing like a cow who has realized her mouth is stuffed with her own product, "I am essentially a foreigner who just passed through New York. You scared of me now?"

"You're not a foreigner; you're American."

"I am a foreigner over there."

"Of course," she said with agitation. Feeling defensive, she reached for a grape, but couldn't find the one she was looking for. After fondling several, she settled for a small one. "And I am glad you got stopped. It should be random; it's not like I am racist or anything. I just want to feel safe." She changed her mind about the grape. Examining it up close, she smashed it between her fingers. "Did you read that article I

140

forwarded, about biological weapons? This stuff is for real, you know."

With the authority of an eldest sister, Inise slurred in her law professor tone, "But, what everyone wants to know, of course, is 'will we trade liberty for security?'"

Cate looked at the rug, shoulders fuming as her feet practiced different angles. She had always felt inferior to Inise, and her sister's fancy degree hadn't helped. But just because Cate was in real estate, didn't mean she was an idiot.

Dragging boredom, Samantha came in and wrapped her arms around her mother's hips. Inise passed the mug to Mac and focused on running her fingers through her daughter's hair. She continued her speech, as if reciting a poem. "There is only so much you can do to safeguard something before you cut off all the air and kill the very life you are trying to protect." And in her own sharp voice, she faced her sister again, "You are a mother. You must know this."

With the mention of motherhood, Cate was no longer the little sister. Her chest and chin rose with fury, "Exactly. I am a *mother*. I take and expect every precaution to be taken. I have three little boys and my husband to worry about. Our safety should at least be secure; that is all I ask."

Inise broke eye contact, and looked back down at Samantha's head. The hair shone a dark hue, Slade's best feature, but it was the ears' activity that worried Inise. Choosing the words carefully, she said, "Nothing is 'secure'. *Life* is change."

Cate continued to glare at her sister, but slowly the scowl was enlightened with pity. That hug was all her sister had; everything for her had "changed." A failed marriage, an ailing career, even the child would eventually grow up and leave her…

"How's the Brie?" She shrugged toward her younger brother.

"Good."

Samantha looked up from her mother's hip.

Spreading some cheese on a cracker with a knife Mac hadn't noticed, Cate reached out, "Want to try some Brie, Samantha?"

"No." Samantha knocked her head back against her mother's hipbone and closed her eyes.

Cate straightened up, her hand now awkwardly full. With Mac watching, she shoved the cholesterol into her mouth and walked away still chewing.

Chapter Twenty-Six

Before daybreak, a new grandmother held a red baby to her chest. He was just two handfuls of human; spindly limbs curled up from a hairy back. His head was enlarged with rage.

The woman sat cross-legged on the floor and clucked with excitement. Her few wrinkles had experienced most of the births in the village, and, each time, her faith had been reinforced by the emergence of an irreplaceable life.

And this birth was an intimate miracle, reverberating from her own traumatic bloodletting twenty-years prior. She was proud of the vitality in his screams. She couldn't see him in this early dawn light, but she felt his fury, his cold, his damp discomfort. She stroked his arm with her thumb and carefully avoided touching the umbilical cord, which had just been tied off with straw. His pulse trembled. Determined.

Rocking, calming him a bit, she tuned past her charge to the rest of the room. She could hear desperation in the midwife's movements.

There was shouting for palm leaves and cloth, panicked shuffling, short whispers, and she recognized, with horror, that her daughter was draining onto the mud floor.

The baby screamed and clawed at the woman's blouse, trying in vain to find a nourishing nipple. The young grandmother cooed mechanically, listening for sighs from her daughter. She heard herself called for, and froze. She felt helpless as a mother; what could she do for her daughter? Maybe as a grandmother…

Her daughter disappeared into silence, as the woman pulled her emotions from the bedside, to the raucous sob in her arms.

Five days later, in full daylight, outside a neighbor's hut, she dutifully presented the tiny human to Radath. She knew he was supposed to get vaccinations. Radath squeezed oil from a blue vitamin into the mouth of the sleepy boy, as she asked about his mother. The grandmother shook her head; her daughter's body had not survived. It lost too much blood. She returned to Radath a sandwich baggy of iron tablets. Thank you but these just made her queasy.

Radath looked at the bag as if it was the corpse of the woman herself. No more than three of the pills were missing from its original sixty. The pregnant woman hadn't understood their importance; they would have prevented the hemorrhaging.

She looked at the skinny infant. "How will you feed him?"

The woman pointed to a can on the low table. Sweetened and condensed milk. It had accompanied the tea the village volunteer presented Radath earlier that morning. The teddy bear on the label leered at the medic. She shook her head, and the bear regained its smile.

Radath sighed, and reiterated the importance of breast milk. Canned milk does not have anywhere close to all the nutrients the baby needed to thrive. Could a nursing mother be found? The grandmother

144

knew one, but didn't think the woman would have enough milk for two babies. She would ask.

Radath took the boy's coin-width forearm and grazed the skin with a needle. An ever so slight angle and the boy was vaccinated. A white circle rose up on his flat red skin. He shook with anger.

Chapter Twenty-Seven

"But what was it about her?' Ria asked.

He had forgotten those pictures were in there. *"What was it about her?" How to explain?* How to say, especially to Ria, that they had bonded over luck and ideals, wanting to give back to the world that had given them so much? That they had hoped in the process they would prove themselves worthwhile, good deeds accumulating like cash in a businessman's bank account. That when he talked of ambition and responsibility, she talked of personal peace. And when she talked of duty and guilt, he railed about the benefits of simplicity. That they shared a cause. How to say any of this, especially to Ria?

"What was is about her?" Was it how she got rolled up in the Sunday paper, looking like a blond smudge of newsprint, lost among the folds, worried that she would know more about how to teach, than about what to teach? Or how she would listen with checked awe to his studies,

his string of chemical acronyms, her belly laugh at hearing VAD is battled by VAC? The blossom of her smile?

No. It was the steady stare that arrived parallel his, at the pause of conversation. The stare deep ahead into the next decades, preparing to understand how to love as many, and as much, as possible. The kisses in the middle of the brow, between the eyebrows, washing away thought. The soft squeeze of her flesh, thighs flashing pale gold in the morning's sunlight, turning pale moon at night. And the wet pungent home he found when he grabbed her pink buttocks and pushed deeper and deeper into the support of her fertile walls.

How to reveal he had found something worth sharing and lost it? How to even see it himself?

"What do you mean?" Taking the photo album out of Ria's hands, Mac tried to change the subject. "Do you want some more coffee?" He got up and walked into the kitchen.

"I mean, you look different in those photographs," she called after him.

Pretending he couldn't hear her clearly through the partition, he yelled, "That's all the pictures I have of the United States. Do you have any from here? Or any from Thailand?"

When he returned, her chest had caved. "I want to know more about your life."

"And I want to know more about yours," he mimicked, handing her a cup of coffee. She stared at the spoon, while he leaned back, noisily stirring his own cup.

Finally, sighing, she explained what he already knew. "I don't have any pictures."

"Well, I've been meaning to get a photography book on Cambodian iconography. Maybe you can help explain some of the stories to me."

Ria stirred her coffee, watching the condensed milk thicken the liquid in splotchy gradations. She stared at it until the spinning stopped. Finally, she looked away and took a sip.

Chapter Twenty-Eight

Mac heard Cate, with a full mouth, loudly offer to help their mother in the kitchen. Inise and her daughter, mumbling within the nest of their arms, wandered off to settle on the couch. Mac was left alone with the snacks. Another couple of dry crackers, and *I should go see Dad before I shower.*

Still chewing, a new stack of crackers in his right hand, mug of gin in his left, Mac entered the back study to find his trim cousin perched on the edge of a sofa, charitably dangling questions in front of Mac's father. Dad looked tired. Especially the left side of his face. *But then again, Lyle can tire anyone out.*

Lyle noticed him first and stood for a proper handshake. Mac made an awkward grasp of crackers and mug in his left hand, brushed crumbs against his pant leg, and received his young cousin's hand. "How you doing there, Lyle?"

"Just fine."

"How's Harvard?"

"Good," he said, nodding plastically, still standing.

"Take your exams yet?"

"They make us wait 'til after Christmas to take them."

"Oh, that's evil."

"Tell me about it." He sat back down and crossed his legs. "But it gives me a good excuse to come visit all of you here, instead of going home to California."

"Uh huh. Hey, Dad. Merry Christmas."

"Merry Christmas, Mac. It is good to see you home." He raised a suddenly thin arm to give him a hug; it shook and Mac swooped down to take over. His father's muscles didn't seem to properly clothe his back, *but he was thinner last year too*, and Mac smelled faulty digestion in his breath. His father's voice, however, was unchanged.

"How you feeling, Dad?"

"Oh fine. The left side is only at eighty percent but it is getting better." His father severed eye contact. "I'm-sure-I'll-be-good-as-new-soon-enough. Did you know that Lyle here is following in your footsteps?"

"Oh yeah? You want to do development work?"

"I want to be a doctor."

"Right…" Mac looked back at his father, eyebrows hiccupping forward.

"I told him you've had plenty of experience in the medical field."

"I guess you could say that. I am going to go shower."

"I think that's a good idea, son. What are you doing, fermenting new cures in those armpits of yours?"

150

Lyle looked stricken. Mac's mouth spread wide. *There's Dad.* "Yeah, I guess I shouldn't sacrifice all of you to my amateur experiments."

"I certainly don't remember signing any consent form, son."

Mac exhaled a short laugh, but before he could banter back, his mother entered, absorbed, "Mel! You haven't even touched your tea!"

Mac escaped behind her, without being noticed.

Chapter Twenty-Nine

It was his maid's day off and Mac had had the day to himself to prepare. In his kitchen, he opened the blue Bombay and poured it over bottled-water ice cubes. He actually had fresh limes today. He got several out for ready serving. He was hoping to offer Chanroth a drink when they arrived. He probably wouldn't accept. *Should I have coffee ready too?*

He found the coffee-bean grinder behind a dish rack. *Should I have offered to help move her? She didn't seem to want me at Chanroth's; sounds like things are going pretty badly over there.* The ground beans dusted the air with a rich smell.

He put the kettle on and added a splash of tonic to his gin. He was on his second drink and the coffee was cold before they arrived.

Chanroth hopped out of his employer's car with a face of stone. From the backseat, he shouldered Ria's single suitcase and walked solidly toward Mac's entrance. Ria sighed from the passenger seat and leaked out of the door with a bulging bamboo handbag.

Why did she need help if that's all there is?

At his stoop, Ria smiled at Mac's window. Mac backed away and greeted Chanroth at the door.

"Hi there. Come on in. Thanks a lot for helping." Mac tried to take the round suitcase but Chanroth held tight. He walked past Mac, and delivered it to the dining-room table.

"I will always help Ria," he said with a forced but steady stare.

*What is that? A threat? Hey, dude, this was all her idea...*A night lying in bed, encouraging her to tell him what would make her happy, hoping for sexual direction. But, it turned out, what would really turn her on, she confessed, would be having her clothes next to his in a closet. "I am always here anyway," came her logic. "It will be easier for me." And Mac had to agree. It would be easier to just have her here, instead of arranging to pick her up, meeting her somewhere, wearing out a chaperone.

She appeared in the doorway.

"Here she is!" Mac was practically shouting. "Is that everything? I think this is cause for celebration. Can I get you two a drink?"

Ria beamed at his excitement and nodded at the drink.

"I have to drive back," Chanroth dampened.

"OK, then, how 'bout a coffee at least?"

"All right," he conceded, looking at Ria.

She moved toward the kitchen to prepare the glasses, but Mac interrupted her. "Why don't you two make yourselves at home in the living room? I will bring out the drinks."

Ria smiled at him and said to Chanroth, "Come see the living room; the windows are really pretty in there."

Across Mac's shoulders, anxiety chased gin. *What have I done?* Chanroth's judgment sped Mac's doubt. For defense, he did a quick shot in the privacy of the kitchen. He put a cup of coffee in the microwave and loaded a rattan tray with sweetened and condensed milk, tonic water, two glasses of ice with lime, and the bottle of Bombay. *Hey Chanroth, she is a big girl; she can make her own decisions. I am not misleading her.*

He triumphantly got the tray to the coffee table without shaking it too much. He had even remembered an honorary saucer for Chanroth's coffee. He made the gin and tonics at the table, in accordance with established preferences, putting as much tonic in Ria's as gin in his. Chanroth reached for the milk can and led a thick stream to puddle at the bottom of his mug. Ria was up and on her way to the kitchen before Mac had even realized what he had forgotten. Mac smiled meekly at Chanroth.

"So, how's the new job going?" he tried.

"Fine." Pause. And then, reconsidering, "How is your job?"

"Fine, I guess. Nothing new."

"Why did you come here again?" Ria reentered and handed Chanroth a spoon. Both men watched her cross close to Mac's chair, taking tiny steps, calf grazing the low table, to regain her seat on the couch.

"This is a beautiful country."

"If I could be in America, I would be."

Oh, here it is. Visa jealousy. Is it my fault that I can ride my passport and currency anywhere in the world while you wait, in vain, for lottery luck? I know it's not fair, but is it MY fault? "But this is such an intriguing place. You have such a rich history; it makes us orphaned Americans jealous."

154

"I don't believe you. Anyway, Americans can see our history, if they want; I don't get to see your 'no history.'"

"Oh, but I am sure I will never understand the beauty of this place to the same degree as you do," Mac coddled. "I really find this place mesmerizing."

"You've been to Angkor."

Let's pretend that was a question. "Only once, but I didn't see enough. I hope to go back sometime." He refreshed the gin in his glass and checked Ria's; she had taken two sips. She was blinking at him excitedly.

"I did my monkhood near there. It was an easy way to improve my English, talking to all you Westerners about Angkor."

Mac felt relieved slightly by the neutral turn of conversation. Nearly all young men in Cambodia had spent some time as a monk. Kind of like gap year in Europe or temporarily joining the military in Israel, it was considered part of the standard course of maturation, and the education received there significantly helped the country's literacy rate. It was also a good place to ride out a bout of unemployment. "How long did you stay in the *sangha*?"

"Two years; until I was fifteen. Most of my friends only joined for a few months, but I stayed; I was learning more in my robes talking to foreigners, than I could have at school."

"Wow. I don't think I could ever be a monk, even for a few months. I would get homesick for gin." Only Ria joined his laugh.

"Well, some people take the vows more seriously than others." Chanroth sounded bored, as if he had repeated this all on countless occasions. "The-hardest-part-for-me-was-not-eating-after-noon."

"Did you study any Buddhism while you were there?"

"A little."

"Do you still worship Buddha?"

155

"We pay our respects to Buddha; we don't worship him."

"Oh that's interesting," Mac heard himself say, suddenly feeling slightly tipsy. *Maybe this Chanroth isn't such a bad guy after all.* Fishing from his almost-forgotten mythology studies, Mac asked, "Can you explain to me how the Buddhists here feel about the Hindu influence?"

"What do you mean?"

"I mean Vishnu reincarnating himself as everybody, from Rama to Siddhartha."

"I don't think it really matters."

"Well, my favorite at Angkor, even among all the Hindu influences, was Bayon." *See, I'm on your side, Buddha man.* "The Bodhisattva faces are astounding."

"I think that's all from a different sect of Buddhism than we study now. Not that it really matters. Besides, I don't really know much about it; there weren't many teachers around when I was in the sangha."

Oh, right, why can I always recall this one fact with such eerie precision; only three thousand out of sixty-five thousand monks survived the almost four years of Khmer Rouge rule.

Ria jumped in with the grace of a diplomat. "It's the local spirits that really matter, but most people just pray to everybody and anybody." She was only half-joking.

"See, this place is so interesting. All the history just mixes up together."

"It is you foreigners who try to separate it all under different names," Chanroth accused.

"So, you see, I am here because I have so much to learn from you, from people here. I could ask you hundreds of questions and still not fully understand."

"Like what exactly?" Chanroth asked, challenging what he perceived as condescension.

156

The gin had fully, and suddenly, caught up with Mac. And he had not expected to be asked for specifics. He stuttered, searching, "Well, like, how, I will never understand, like…how can places like Angkor Wat and Tuol Sleng exist in the same country?" *What did I just say? Insensitive bastard.* "I mean, do they balance each other or something like…" he continued, but in trying to backpedal, the sentence lost its coordination. Mac fervently wished he wasn't the only one drunk.

Chanroth was staring at Ria. Her hair fell in black rivers down the sides of her face and her eyelids were cast down like protective shells. Peering passively at the rug through the ocular of her glass, she held the drink dutifully forward, perching delicate elbows upon tightly pressed knees. The sunlight streamed in from the window to play with the tiny bones in her hand.

Chanroth shrugged, and answered Mac's question with his own question. "How can love and hate be felt by the same heart?"

Chapter Thirty

In his turn out of his father's study, out through its alternative door into the living room, determined to finish his search for a shower, the centripetal force was too great and he had to use the wall to steady himself.

Man, that gin went straight to my head.

The couch on the other side of the room unfolded itself, burying Inise, Samantha, and *The Brothers Grimm*. In its place, a separate vision appeared. He saw a timid version of himself sprawled across the couch bed, enduring a painful rod down the middle of his back. The sheets quivered from the fondling ecstasy occurring underneath. He heard her muffled breath. Quiet sweating.

Mac closed his eyes, hand still against the wall. The strokes became palpable. Mac smelled her, squirming pungent honey, and found himself falling, too fast, air roaring over his ears, into her placid stare.

And then it all grew wet, a dark humidity puddling under his eyelids, a trickle going over the top of his lip…

…a drop landing squarely in the fold of the map between his hands. Georgia looked up, past him, to the sky and then down into her bag. Bashfully, she pulled out an umbrella.

"You have an umbrella?" It didn't fit her projected image, that of a pixie, irresponsible and carefree.

"Um, yeah, it seems that I do." Guilty, caught, but then, trying to boost her value as his companion, she added, "I usually have an umbrella."

"Really?"

"Yeah, when there are plans I really want to do." She beamed at him. "You hold the map and I'll hold the umbrella." She opened it up, almost hitting a Thai man holding a newspaper over his head. She stretched her mouth in apology but the man rushed off, familiar with the nuisance of tourists. She sent Mac a look of embarrassment. "I guess I'll have to work on the opening part."

Mac laughed and bent down for a quick, culturally inappropriate, kiss. Their saliva met briefly between pursed flesh and Mac felt shaken. He had bent down for a sparkle and got a lightning bolt instead. Clearing his throat into the map, "Um, so now we don't have to find a museum; we can go anywhere."

"That's the idea."

"Where do you want to go?"

"Everywhere. With you."

He looked at her. Her bangs were hugging her face, becoming darker in the dampness, and her skin was already dewy. Her cheeks were still flushed with the hotel sex they'd had a few hours earlier. He could feel the echo of her body on his, could still see those soft shoulders, without that bag and tank top, pulsing. Her eyes were feasting on his

159

image too, and the temples and Buddhas seemed irrelevant. He was so happy, it scared him. He wanted to trust her completely; *can I?*

"What about when I am too old to read a map?"

"Well, hopefully we won't need a map, or an umbrella, by then," she replied, swaying in the same happiness. "By then, we probably won't even be able to do stairs. We'll only need to find our way to a couch bed on a ground floor."

"Umm, a couch bed with you," *that hand-job...*"that's the way to go."

"Everywhere. With you." He knocked his mug against the TV set, setting it down hard against the cheeks still flushing in his memory.

Liar; Two-faced Liar. He slimed the words all over her image, smearing her mouth, rubbing them into her nostrils, scooping deep from a pit of rancid nausea. He tried to smother her, erase her into little pieces of rolled-up debris, but her face remained, following him, mocking him with that ever-dissipating smile. In retaliation, he spit acid on her brow and cheekbones; it seared and sizzled but she didn't react. The smile remained. Into the saliva mist, he hissed: *Liar.*

He found crackers in his hand and stacked them next to his mug. A churning rose to his throat as he walked past his sister and niece without a word. He took to the stairs like a rescue ladder. His sister looked at the crackers on the TV set, tried to understand them, and then returned her stare to the book in her daughter's lap.

On the second floor, in the safe humidity of his mother's bathroom, the nausea condensed upward to only dew his lashes. *That was all a long time ago. A lot has happened since then.*

160

Unbuckling his belt, his pants dropped to the floor. His shirt peeled off his back. *I do stink.* He carried an unfamiliar belly behind the plastic curtain and subjected it to a scalding waterfall. The resulting fog on the mirror gave a more accurate reflection of any recent self he remembered.

Chapter Thirty-One

His desk was already clear. He usually left it messy but here it is, already clear. He even had his keys in his pocket. He swiveled the chair from one corner to the next, simulating the pacing he was too tired to do. His watch seemed stuck just after seven.

What can I do to waste a little time? I am already so tired. I want my bed. But can I just walk past her? Ria will want conversation. Sex. It is too early to claim fatigue.

He took some articles out of his desk. Things he had been trying to finish reading—updates, now a few months old, on Golden Rice. He was already familiar with the basic story. Eighty percent of the average Cambodian's daily calories was made up of rice; seemed like a good idea to imbue it with some vitamins. But everyone in his field was in tizzy. "It is not the best solution."

"But," Mac's handwriting argued down the margins of the first article, *"no one in the 1900s looked at a Great Lakes schoolgirl, her*

adolescent neck swelling large on one side with goiter, and said, "Well we could look into a way of adding iodide to your food, so you and your future children don't have to suffer, but there are potential risks, so why don't you just wait until you can afford a more diverse food supply…" American children grow up with fortified everything, bread, baby food, milk, cereal. But alter a gene, make the fortification able to be passed on to the next crop, and everyone freaks. Altering chemical structure, i.e., iodized salt, was freaky at one time too…"

In the bottom border of the second page, *"Of course, we don't know all the potential ramifications…But what is more tragic, possible cancer at seventy or guaranteed blindness at age five? Honestly, which does more harm to the economy?"*

And on the back side, *"True, the vitamin capacity of GR is not yet sufficient. But could it be, eventually?"*

He needed to have a defendable opinion on this subject; his job required it. Fired up and ambitious, the newbies he hired to send out into the field, to do the work he used to do, would ask him. His colleagues would debate him. *Do the benefits outweigh the dangers…? How come no one seems to like this? Am I not understanding something? Will this phase me out of a job? I feel like I only know vitamin A anymore.*

The anger in the months-old handwriting made him homesick. *I miss Georgia. Stop it. You've been doing this without her for years now. Last year, you were just fine.*

He evened the pile of articles like a stack of cards, looking for luck with one hopeful knock against his desk. He cleared his throat, trying to get his own attention, and hovered his face above the pages. The words swirled into a paisley pattern. He shook his head. The pattern only kaleidoscoped.

Leaning back in his chair as he rubbed his eyes, his other hand grabbed the handle off the phone.

163

"Hi, yeah, it's me…Tired." He stopped rubbing his eyes and the phone switched hands. "Do we have anything there to eat, other than rice?" He rubbed a finger up and down the rim of his desk. "No, don't make me anything. I'll grab some dumplings on the street," he said, talking into his lap. "It was fine; yours? OK, I'll be home soon."

Leaving the office door open to light the hallway, he wandered down to the lounge they called the lunchroom. It had been two hours since the house had emptied for the day and this room still smelled of instant noodles. He opened the midget fridge next to the water cooler. It was the only light he bothered to turn on. He took the peanut butter jar out. In oil-smeared marker, the label announced his ownership. He grabbed the similarly labeled crackers off the table jutting out from the other-side of the fridge. The double pack was a third empty; it had been almost full earlier. Mac shrugged, *go ahead, eat my crackers, got more in my desk…*

Leaning on the fridge top, he pushed crackers into the peanut butter jar. They pulled out easily covered; the fridge was barely functional. Saltines broke against his tongue and relinquished the peanut butter. Crisp. Unctuous. Until there were no more crackers. His desk was too far away. He was not hungry anyway. Mac reached his finger into the jar. He ran it against the side and rim. The peanut butter rippled up, daring him. Sticking the finger in his mouth, he immediately sucked at the finger's webbing, cleaning away the last traces of peanut butter. Miraculously, he left it at that. Just one finger dip was all he would be allowed; he had been putting on too much weight recently. *Well maybe one more.* And another. His throat soothed the butter down, and his stomach protested feebly. The lid went on. And then off, for one more dip. On. And then off…

The light went out with the closure of the fridge door. He rubbed the saliva-sticky hand against his pant leg as he hunched against the darkness, toward the spotlight of his office. The papers on his desk were swept into his briefcase, as if he would read this trash at home.

He tipped the motorcycle taxi, and sniffed deep into the exhaust that had gathered on his shirt collar. He tried to suck the poison inside.

Ria opened the door for him before he could even reach his stoop. She was holding a little plate. A sticky cake of sweetened rice. She looked pretty. Her hair had been neatly arranged on the top of her head. Her makeup was done in careful gradations of pink, reaching their pinnacle at her mouth. Her bare arms had been powdered whiter. *It must be the powder that makes her always smell of frosting.*

She greeted him with the plate. He bared his teeth, "Oh how sweet." *Again, my avoidance of sugar is ruined.*

He stuffed the palm-sized cake into his mouth, two bites and it was gone, before he had even set down his briefcase.

He did his lines, "Oh, it's delicious. Did you make this yourself?"

She nodded, staring at him, as he had instructed, instead of at her hands. "How was your day?"

"Long. I am very tired. And I still have some more work to do."

Her chin fell with his announcement of more work. They hadn't had sex in three weeks and Ria needed sex with him like food. She deflated a little more every day that went by without it. They got by on her English, but sex was the only real way they communicated; how else could she know if she was still wanted?

He used to let her go down on him whenever she wanted. "Yeah, anytime; it's better than masturbating," he had drunkenly declared. But lately he had been softly posturing his way out. Only in the morning did

165

she find him hard, when his alarm woke them both up, and he swore and groaned at the existence of another day.

"I'm gonna go take a shower," he said and escaped the foyer.

She prepared tea and arranged it carefully in the living room for him, near his favorite chair. She put his flask in easy reach.

The door of the bathroom opened, and Ria adjusted her posture, squeezing her arms around her chest, to give her small breasts a seductive lift, while simultaneously trying to look both innocent and relaxed.

The door to the bedroom opened and shut. She then realized he had taken the briefcase in with him. She ran the hot water through the metal filter. His mug filled green and steaming.

Mac let the towel fall to the ground and donned boxers under his belly. Carrying the briefcase to the floor near the bed, he sat and began rummaging with her approach. This routine had already gotten old.

As she placed his mug on the nightstand, he noticed her skirt was shorter today. She had on an American-style tank top, the kind with only tiny spaghetti straps. She looked annoyingly attractive. He smiled his thank you, fed her the compliment, and looked through the articles he had recovered. Encouraged, she crawled in next to him. Seconds disappeared as he settled back and pretended to read.

"What are you reading?"

"Just some articles for work."

"What's Golden Rice?"

"It's a rice that has a vitamin precursor in it."

"Why is it golden? Is it expensive?"

"It's yellow. It has a daffodil gene in it. Would you eat yellow rice if it was good for you?"

166

"Yellow?" She wrinkled her nose and shook her head. "Rice that isn't white is for animals. Anyway, I prefer bread," she stated decidedly, although Mac had witnessed the opposite.

"Oh that's just because you like to pretend you are French."

"What's wrong with pretending I am French?" She ran her hand up his inner thigh.

"Nothing," he whispered as she found his boxer-clad sack. He closed his eyes, willing himself hard. He thought of the mole made visible on her breast when she had bent over to deliver his tea. The accessibility of her near skirt. Her knee passed over his as she wrapped herself around his thigh, playfully placing kisses everywhere below the limp penis. It stirred and they both got excited. She licked his balls through the opening in the boxer shorts, watching his member grow. Rolling over to his side, she slowly started to inch the elastic band down. He gulped and put his hand on her back. Under the thin tank top, he could feel birdlike bones and a rib cage knotted together at the spine. He went soft.

Frustrated, he hid his face under the papers that had dropped to his chest, "Installing a Glass Ceiling in the Third World: Europe Won't Buy Genetically Modified Produce," and moved a hand to stroke her hair and ear. She too pretended nothing had happened. Next to the warmth of his hip, she secured herself in a tight fetal position, ducking her forehead into her own body.

Chapter Thirty-Two

Coming back down the stairs, a draft chilled the water on his scalp and confirmed a trickle on his neck.

I can't even dry my hair right.

He pulled at the sweater he hadn't worn since last Christmas, trying to stretch it a size bigger.

Reaching the bottom, he was not sure what to do with himself. He felt confronted by the door to the outside, the way a prisoner must feel attacked by his bars. *It is already six thirty. We will eat soon. The kids will make sure of it.*

Lyle and Cate were in the kitchen, ostensibly talking to Mom. Mac saddled through, grabbing a canister of fried onion topping from the counter.

"Mac," Lyle tried to include him, "I was just telling Cate that I hope, once I graduate from Harvard, I hope to enter a PhD/MD program. That way I can do research *and*—"

"Mac, don't eat all those, OK? They are for the green bean casserole."

"Don't worry, Mom," he assured her, peeling the lid back and settling into a chair at the kitchen table.

Cate's eyes bounced on from Mac, "It's a good idea, Lyle. People always need doctors; you'll always be in demand. But, like, for me, people just aren't buying houses right now. It doesn't matter how good of a saleswoman I am, I can't sell to thin air…"

"Yeah, that has to be hard, to have your profession tied to the economy like that."

Vindicated, Cate altered her gaze to more aggressively include her mother in the conversation, "And if Greg doesn't get this promotion, I don't know what we are going to do." She fingered the already-folded napkins, stacking them neatly yet again.

"All I want to do is take good care of my family…" she added, glancing at Mac, as her eldest son ran to her thigh.

"Can we play soccer in the living room? If we be real careful?"

With a sultry shine, a platinum watch whined down her forearm to nestle on his hair. For a moment, a snarl in the boy's hair became caught between the links. "Go ask your father."

Mac focused on the crispy fried curls, folding the breading against his tongue.

"And I don't think the kids should have to give up soccer."

"Of course not. Competition is good for kids; why, when I was younger—"

Cate was liking her cousin more and more, "And Greg just doesn't understand how expensive women's clothes are. People won't trust me if I show up in ratty clothes from last season."

Mom nodded at her, while handing her a stack of plates, "Can you put these on the table?"

Cate grumpily pivoted on her heel. Lyle continued to Mac, "But it's weird, isn't it? The PhDs don't like the MDs and the MDs don't like the PhDs…"

The onion circles crunched in his mouth dryly. The noise tastelessly drowned his cousin out. *How do they do it? Exist; want?* Mac was chewing only to be part of the scene; the only thing he really wanted was to stop existing. It was not the future that looked hostile; it was the present that felt violently dull.

Lyle, flailing in the mal-attention, reached for the napkins and sheepishly followed Cate's exit. Cate returned without him. Her two older boys trailed instead, "Dad said to ask you."

"Well, then I say no."

"But Maa'om, it is already dark outside."

"Tom, what did I say about whining? You are too old for that now."

"Mommy," the younger one indulged in the baby voice his brother was just reprimanded for, "Can I have some stocking candy?"

"No, we are going to eat soon." Cate looked at her mother.

"I am sorry; I will be done in just a…." Their mother turned away from basting the roast. She made a confused circle. "I just wasn't sure what time Mac would be here. Mac, did you get those caramels? I have to finish dessert."

"Oh yeah." He tossed another fried onion into his mouth, pasting his mouth with breading, as he rose from his chair. Heavily, he pressed back up the stairs to rummage in his bag.

Cate settled the boys in front of a tape of cartoons. In high-pitched awe, the songs welcomed all children, young and old, far and near, worldwide (!), to list US states and capitals.

170

Inise drowsily asked her to turn down the volume. "Samantha is reading."

Cate returned to the kitchen. "What are we having for dessert?" she asked suspiciously.

"Crumb cake. I think I will melt caramel on top."

"Crumb cake? Do you know how much butter they put in that?"

"Not off hand. I got it from the grocery store, but I am sure I could find a recipe for you."

"No." Cate stared at her. "You know the topping on that stuff is just butter and sugar," she accused. "Do we have some fruit at least? That much cholesterol can't be good for Dad."

Rounding the bottom of the stairs, Mac heard Cate's last sentence. He charged toward her silhouette in the doorway, brandishing an interruption, "This-is-all-I-could-find-Mom."

She looked at the caramels, pupils narrowing, eyes wet, as she saw the white-paste swirls. The filling would ruin everything. "I can't melt those, Mac!" She looked at Mac, stricken, refusing all eye contact with Cate.

"Mom!" He felt frantic; he was trying to save her, but here she looked stabbed by his own sword, "Mom, I didn't know…" *Melting? Why is this such a big deal?* "But your pies are always so delicious! They don't need any caramel!"

She took the cellophane packages out of his hands, staring in disbelief, wondering how she would now make the store-bought cake "special" and if Cate blamed her cooking for her father's stroke. Slowly, Mac's voice filtered through her ears. "Oh, Mac, I'm sorry." She looked up at him, shrinking by the moment, "I didn't make any pies!"

Mac watched his mother puddle in front of him, and felt like a perverse Dorothy melting the wrong witch. Grabbing his gut, he said,

"Oh thank god, the last thing my belly needs is to be tempted by your pies."

But she didn't laugh. Her wrinkles deepened with concern and apology. "But I have crumb cake. You'll eat crumb cake, won't you?" Her mouth traced over the sentence again, quivering as she awaited the verdict.

"Crumb cake! I love crumb cake!"

"But what are we going to do with those?" Cate pointed to the packages that had somehow ended up back in Mac's hand.

Like a dog responding to a pitched whistle, Tony entered the kitchen again for another attempt, hoping the extra voice would make it harder for his mother to say no. "Maaaa'hmy, I am really huuuun'gry. Lyle said to ask you if I can have a snack."

Cate was opening her mouth, but Mac was already on his knees, wanting to remedy everything, "Hungry, eh? Well then, I have the perfect Christmas present for you."

Tony was off, calling to his brother, bragging about the treasure of candy that had just fallen into his lap, before Mac could even stand back up.

Cate barked after him, "Tony, you share with your brother." And then to Mac, "Next time, ask me before doing something like that. I don't let them have sugar before dinner."

"Oh, Cate, come off it," Inise said, entering the kitchen and yawning into her siblings' faces. "We used to eat candy all day on Christmas. And we turned out fine."

"Oh, good, Inise, I am glad you are awake. I need your help with the rolls; I am gonna start the potatoes now, so we are almost done."

"I thought I smelled something yummy," Inise said, peeking in at the roast and rescuing a drippings-drowning carrot. She noticed her mother dangling a plastic bag of ready-to-bake roll dough in front of her.

She snatched it, surveying the woman in disbelief. Her mother's eyes were darting all over the kitchen.

Finding a groove in the ceiling to focus on, as if that was where she would find the potato masher, her mother announced, "And your father still hasn't opened the wine."

"I'll do it," Cate and Mac said simultaneously, shouldering up.

"Well, I think we'll need two bottles anyway…" she mollified, a little unnerved by their ready cooperation.

Cate and Mac moved to the dining room. There were snacks still littering the arrangement of plates, napkins, and a pinecone/flower bouquet. The table still lacked silverware and simplicity before Mom would deem it worthy of food, but Cate and Mac were now in a race to see who could get a bottle open first.

"No fair; you have the better opener."

"Wanna switch?" Mac, suddenly tired again, wished he could just let her do both of them.

"No, it doesn't matter."

Mac's cork popped out, but Cate's slid noiselessly free at almost the same time. It was impossible to tell which was first, but Cate looked smug.

Their father called out from the study, "Hey, is that wine I hear?"

"Well, you're not supposed to hear wine, but in this house, apparently you do. Want some, Dad?"

"Uh huh, and some of those crackers, while you're at it."

Cate did a little graceful weight shift, as she filled her father's glass, and then, handing Mac the plate of crackers, waltzed solo into the study. Mac followed stupidly behind.

Two sips of wine, four crackers, and Dad looked happy. Mac couldn't wait for this holiday to be over. Cate sat on the ottoman and smiled up at her father.

"Well, Mac, it is good to see you, son."

"Thanks, Dad, it is good to be seen, I guess."

"So when are you going to come back here, where you belong?"

"You mean to the States?"

"Yeah, you've been out there long enough, haven't you? You must be done sowing your wild oats by now," his father teased in masked concern. "I imagine you are getting ready to take on something more permanent."

"I have a permanent position there, Dad."

"Oh I know, and it is good to get some traveling under your belt, but a grown *man* belongs at home, don't you think?"

"I feel at home there too."

"Of course you say that. What do you like about that barren place anyway?"

"It's not barren—"

"Oh, Dad, leave him alone," Cate interrupted Mac. "He just wants to be where no one reminds him of Georgia."

Mac imagined his own wine glass smashing into Cate's cheekbone, shattering into splinters, blood streaking from eye cavity to nose crevice, slices smarting with alcohol, as Mac doubled over with giggles.

Chapter Thirty-Three

It was Saturday morning. Ten o'clock. Ria had been out of bed for hours. He even heard her leave, bamboo flip-flops and key jangle, only to have the sounds return an hour later, accompanied by swishing bags.

Mac tried to stretch against gravity but quickly sighed defeat. The sheets were quiet. The pillows accepted him.

In the kitchen, she moved to fill her water glass yet again, and reopened a newspaper with exaggerated sound effects. He knew she was waiting for him to eat breakfast. He was certain that fruit, croissants, and coffee were displayed on the table, being surveyed by flies that braved the current of the ceiling fan. She would have for him today's *Cambodia Daily*, the local English-language news publication. Hers would be in French.

He heard a loud sigh and another rustle. *Why can't she just eat by herself and go out for the day?*

He struggled up, dismayed to discover the weight of his head. In vain, his neck tried to call in sick. Mac pulled a robe, last year's Christmas gift from his sister, around his shoulders and closed it against his boxers. Rubbing the sleep out of his eyes, he was determined to put on a pleasant mask for Ria. *She really is too sweet to me.* "Hello there, sugar."

She looked at him seriously. Hungry. "Ready for some breakfast?"

"Yeah, let me just hit the john first."

"Hit John?"

Why did I say it that way? "Go to the bathroom."

The tile was cool and dry. The open air in the house was already making a sultry contrast to the floor. There was a beautiful sky out the window. He could hear the call of a quail egg peddler plodding down the near road. *I am a very lucky man. One of the luckiest in the world. I should just snap out of this. Really, what do I have to be so damn sad about?*

He joined her at his table and she handed him his paper. As soon as he took a croissant, she grabbed one for herself, opened it up, and poured it deep with syrup.

"You know you don't have to wait for me to eat, right?"

"Yes, you always say 'do whatever I want,' but sometimes what I want is to do things with you."

There was a measurement of rehearsal in her statement. It taunted him, catching in the glimmer of his knife. He pushed back, using the knife to secure some soft Camembert. His stomach burned its now usual morning burn, and cheese would put out the flame.

The front page of the paper held a picture detailing one of the temples at Angkor. Unsurprisingly, the article advertised something about a renewed/ongoing restoration project, and of course, once again,
176

reassured tourists that all land mines had been cleared in the surrounding area. Tourists could travel freely around Angkor, the article promoted, unlike most of the rest of the country, which held somewhere between four and ten million land mines. Two or three of which were discovered every day by blowing the limb off an unsuspecting wanderer. The journalist couldn't control herself: One in every forty-five Cambodians is an amputee.

But something in the picture, in the relief depicting an *apsara*, a temple dancer, held his attention longer than the text possibly could, especially in this ebbing hangover. Her knees were bent in a deeper squat than the other dancers he remembered on other Angkor walls. Her stance seemed closer to the painful position he had watched Indian dancers use, pounding their feet out from under a low torso; these dancers had accompanied the music boldly as if their bodies were additional instruments.

He had sought out Ramayana performances in both countries. And here in Cambodia, there had been more an emphasis on hand gestures, curved and solemn, while in India the emphasis had been on the feet, belled and loud, legs folded for punctuated rhythm. But this Angkor dancer was holding her torso very low, over acutely bent knees, and her feet were large, out of proportion, as if to emphasize their speed.

It was said, in ancient times, gods channeled classical dancers to bring messages to Cambodian kings. The secrecy surrounding true classical dance, traditionally reserved for only royal audiences, had always compounded Mac's curiosity.

"Did you ever take any temple dance?"

"Temple dance?"

"Yeah, like the stuff on the walls at Angkor?"

"No, I didn't work at one of those 'traditional dance' restaurants." She blinked away a sneer, and then quickly added, in an

177

encouraging tone, "We can go see some, if you want. In Siem Reap…"

The air silently pulsed the rest of her statement, the request she had been posturing around for months: *"And visit my father, who will expect you to prove that your intentions toward me are honorable, who will expect you to propose within the following week..."*

"No. I don't want to go to Angkor with you. I am just curious about the differing emphasis of hands and feet on the telling of the Ramayana. Do you know how the choreography is formed?"

With a full mouth, to muffle her annoyance, she chewed the words, "I don't know; maybe they just copy off the walls." Swallowing, she asked, "How was your call with your mother?"

"Fine." The hellos, the how are you, the happy birthday, dear Mo'om, the attempts at jokes thwarted by the awkward long-distance delay between lines of conversation.

"Did she have a nice birthday?"

"I think so." He turned his eyes back to the picture of the temple dancer.

"Are you planning to go back there for Christmas again this year?"

"Yeah. I'll go." He opened the paper to see if there was another picture on the inside with the article's continuation. There was, but here the photographer had focused only on the dancer's upper half. *Breast man, obviously; legs are so underrated.*

Suddenly his paper rippled with the rush of Ria, sobbing past him toward their bedroom.

Shocked, he followed, and found her kneeling, fishing her round suitcase out from under the bed.

In one exasperated breath, she ejected, "I don't understand why you don't want to be with me!"

"What are you talking about? I am with you!"

178

"Many men love me, you know. Many men think me beautiful. Many men want to make me their wife."

He stared at her frozen. His look confirmed all her doubts.

"Do you see her when you go back to the States?"

"Who?"

"The girl in the pictures."

"Georgia?"

She nodded. He laughed, and even to him the laugh came out sounding sinister. He extended it, trying to make it take a more appropriate tone. It was no use. "No. I never see her. *Believe me*, she is not competition for you."

"I don't believe you." She rolled her black pants from a bottom drawer into the suitcase.

"I am telling you the truth. Please stop packing. I don't want you to leave."

"I am going to see my father." She threw a brush and barrette into the open circle. "If you don't come with me, I am not coming back. At least not here," she said, gesturing to his bedroom. She turned her back on him to hide her tears in the closet.

"But I like having you here."

"I am getting too old to just be playing," she hiccupped to the hangers.

"But, Ria, I am not playing. You are important to me; I have so much respect for you..."

"But you never say anything about the future." Wrapping her arm around the clothes, steadying herself, she pulled all three dresses and two blouses off the hangers at once. Burying her face into the pile as she swung past him to her suitcase, she mumbled, "You don't want me; you want my history. You want to rescue me, not love me."

179

Belatedly, he saw their conversations somersaulting down a hill—asking about her culture, her upbringing, her schooling, her stories; about the games he saw between young people in the street, about Theravada versus Mahayana, about iconography, about her ancestors and immediate family, but failing to ask sincerely about her day, her mood, her plans, herself…The somersault ended in a pit, marked by a stamp, a chime of bangs, and a suitcase.

"My name is Ria, not Cambodia."

Chapter Thirty-Four

Their father looked past her and Cate turned to find her brother's shield threatening to knock her out. She recoiled. She hadn't meant to cut that deep. "But I am sure it feels less barren now that you have a girlfriend there," she said, trying to make amends.

Mac looked at the carpet, aware that he had been about to kill. He said nothing. Lyle entered, announcing dinner was on the table.

Cate put her arm under Dad's back, giving him a push forward and then, grabbing his hand, pulled him up. She did so with, what seemed to Mac, an exaggerated amount of flourish. Accented and cur-li-cued, her gestures showed that this technique, so vital to Dad's quality of life, was one Mac didn't know anything about, and it was too complicated to learn in a holiday visit. Dad leaned on her from his left, pretending not to need her support, pretending to just be enjoying his daughter, walking arm in arm. But the grimace on his right side revealed an inner conflict.

Mac followed meekly behind. He scuffed at the floor, hoping it would hold him back, and save him from dinner. He was already dreading the feel of the familiar chair on his butt, and the imprisoning bars at his back. He saw Gram shuffling into the room, framed by the door to the stairs, and knew he was trapped.

But Cate wanted more, wanted him chatting about something happy for once, "So when are you ever going to let us meet—her?" She threw the question over her shoulder, obviously having forgotten Ria's name. Gram looked up at the "her."

Mac halted. He felt doused by Cate's words, words that seemed particularly polluted in Gram's presence. But he couldn't let them just drip away. He couldn't let Cate look the part of the caring, interested sister; he couldn't let her redeem herself after that Georgia comment.

"*Ria*," he corrected loudly, "left me for some silk salesman." Everyone cringed. He had chosen a worthy weapon. "Yeah, some fancy married man who can keep her in an apartment in the boutique section of Phnom Penh while he is in France.

"He visits twice a month, on business, no more, no less," he continued, gleefully spouting information, soaking the table decorations in putrid orange and smearing toothpaste all over the roast beef. "I think she is happy with the setup, but I wouldn't know; she doesn't talk to me anymore."

He came to a full stop. He let all his spew solidify and then waded in the echo to resign himself to his usual seat. *Can we get on with this trash?*

"Oh, I forgot the ladle." His mother valiantly threw the statement out into the room and hurried back into the kitchen.

Lyle followed, with a too loud: "Do you need help with anything else?"

But it was the influx of boys, tumbling in, roughhousing around a frail great-grandmother, that actually succeeded in changing the subject. Gram teetered forward, and grabbed hold of Samantha. Samantha gasped and froze, but, for Gram, the grab reinitiated her shuffle. She arrived at the table mechanically, face stoic, but adrenalin dripped from her ever-moving fingertips. Blue veins rolled over delicate bones. Halted against her chair, she looked at the red bulbs and green wiring Samantha had recycled into napkin holders. Defensively, she shouted, "Why is it Christmas again already!"

"What do you mean, Gram?" Inise entered carrying a casserole dish.

She looked over at the poinsettia and pinecone display that had been moved to a corner of the table. She pointed accusingly.

"But, Gram, aren't there decorations at Sunnyfields?"

"I, I thought they forgot to take them down…" Gram, still standing, looked at her plate quietly. Somehow, she found courage in the porcelain and looked back up, at no one specific, announcing loudly to the entire room, "Well, I'm not giving anyone presents. OK? Sorry." Her jaw set, "I thought we just had Christmas."

Tom and Tony, giggling until the "no presents" bit, looked at her, stunned. "But we've only had Christmas Eve," Tony argued. "Christmas was a whole yeeeaaar ago!"

Greg took over. "You kids got plenty of presents this morning."

"But there's more tonight, right?" Tom looked very concerned.

"Santa left a few presents for you at Grandma's house," Mac's mother pacified.

"But, Grammy doesn't even know it is Christmas!" Tony cried.

"Shhht, you two, Santa is still watching, you know," Cate stepped in. "If you want Christmas to come again next year, you'll cool it right now."

Somewhere in the chaos over presents, Gram bent into her seat. She scowled at the platter holding the roast, as her body ached into a settled position. A tremor in her hand moved to the pearl choker at her throat. Her thumb and forefinger mimed rolling the dark sheen without quite making contact. Her eyes too had lost focus.

Chapter Thirty-Five

Ria watched the excitement in the street from her new balcony. It was a feast. Barely enough, but a feast nonetheless. Being shared among a man and two kids, there were three plastic bags—one with sautéed watercress, another with curried tripe, and the largest one holding a snow-mountain of rice. It must have been bought in the market, running the man up an entire US dollar.

With the bags on the ground, the small family circled and ate with their hands, eyes in steady focus as they balanced on their heels. They were celebrating in the dirt of their missing trash heap, which had been cleared by the government for the holiday.

Ria picked up her hand phone and called her father. They wished each other good health and luck in acknowledgment of the day. She hinted that she would be able to send him money soon, and asked after their adopted "great aunt."

"All she wants to do is grind coriander and green pepper; I catch her going through the motions when she isn't even at the pestle. She grinds much more than I can use here. Might have found a restaurant that will buy some though, to add to their curry mix—"

This was more information than Ria needed; she wanted adjectives, not details. "And how's business?" she interrupted.

Her father got the hint. "Usual."

Slow, Ria interpreted. "I am sure the season will pick up soon."

"Of course."

"Well, Father, I have to get going."

"I know…" This was always the stagnant part. The part in their weekly conversation when he wanted nothing more than to give his only daughter some fatherly advice. But how could he? Everything had changed since her birth. Phnom Penh was unrecognizable, and so was he. He had been an astute engineering professor, a reliable husband, a proud father. Now, he barely had the energy to be a bumbling hotel owner. Caring for the old woman made him feel good about himself. But Ria? Ria he had no idea how to advise. Even his occasional harping about marriage seemed somehow old-fashioned. "Ok, well, um, take care, my dear."

Chapter Thirty-Six

At the table, Dad creaked back down into a sitting position, settling behind a plate, which was stabilized from underneath by a wet washcloth. Mom handed Mac the carving knife. Mac looked across at his father, but Dad didn't look back. Instead, keeping his head focused on his lap, his father decided to say grace.

We never say grace. It's always "come and eat!" "Food! Glorious Food!" But here was Dad, declining his old role and inventing a new job.

"Let us all be grateful for our families and good fortune. On this day of gifts, let us truly enjoy what it is to give."

Mac's limbic system went yellow with phlegm, congealing hard and clamping down on internal organs. It was the familiarity that was the most painful, not the change. He didn't want to see his father this naked. *Come on, please clothe this sentimentality; please, it's just all too blatantly exposed.*

A mumble of confused thanks and agreement spilled forth and dissipated among the place settings.

I guess I'm supposed to stand now, and carve, "give to my family," and all that. But his body had solidified. With desperate fatigue, he pressed against the ground. *Oh, man, am I dizzy.*

Around the table, tied to their chairs, his family looked like blow-up dolls, bobbing, swaying, human flesh grafted on swollen plastic. Gory features jutted from bouncing heads.

Can't they just let me bury myself under the rug, under the table...have all their foot swings and shifts stomp me into oblivion...please.

From each empty plate, a stare pounded into his rusted body, hammering him toward the orange beef. The knife was so heavy he could barely raise it, but he was trying to get through this, trying to salvage his demeanor. He managed to prop the knife between his leaning body and the meat. It pushed against rubber, creating glue instead of friction, and he couldn't get the blade back out again; it was stuck slaying the already twice-dead beast, pathetically protruding like a belated stake. The roast's revenge.

Oh, please don't make me touch this; it knows I am no match for it. Please don't make me see that I can't even...Oh god, what have I done?

Mac backed away from the table, releasing the knife, staring in horror and disbelief at his mother's roast now so impotently impaled. A cool silver point made a horizontal line with its handle, burping in between to exhale pink jus. It was suspended parallel to the table, held static and grotesque in its description of unyielding flesh.

The air was hard in his lungs. He was trying to choke it down, but it escaped with a fast burst, a choking struggle, an explosion against drowning. Swallowing against oxygen, staring at the knife, wanting to be

188

the beef, his chin quivering, nostrils flaring, another rough scraping gasp brought his eyebrows together. Fried onion rose in his throat, as he closed his eyes and succumbed to a decompression of air. In the rushing expansion, his face broke along every fault line, opening wide into the release. Mac fell through the cracks, wind rushing too fast to catch his breath and eyes closed tight, so tight, pressing hard, reprimanding the tears, mouth squeezing back the reflux in his throat...

"Masterson? Are you all right?"

Crumbling, he fell up the stairs, leaving his family gaping at the fixed blade.

In his room, he collapsed like a teenager onto his bed. Shoes on still, dragging dirt onto the comforter, he heard hushed conversation on the floor below. Inise's voice was salient intermittently, loud with drunk volume, "Just let him be, OK?"

He pulled a pillow over his head. He was so tired the room seemed to be spinning, rocking, taking off like a plane, landing, repeat. He finally heard silverware against plates and knew they had carried on like it was Thanksgiving and he wasn't home. He hoped to sleep for the rest of his life.

Waking up at midnight, midday Cambodia time, the house sounded dark, if not quiet. His body felt like lead. Mechanically, he opened up the nightstand, and rummaged under the drawer lining till he found what he had buried there: a newspaper clipping five years old.

Its pages held excerpts from a suicide bomber's diary, headed by a brief bio. The girl, twenty-one, a Hindu from rural South India, had somehow managed to be educated, on scholarship, in Northern India.

Her diary had been found on the ground nearby the bombing area, against the wall surrounding the Taj. It had been wrapped in a large cloth with some other personal items: toothbrush, school identity card, a letter to her mother, a marred barrette. Excerpting from dog-eared pages, the article translated the diary's Hindi:

"The Taj Mahal, the opulent palace, the place of undying romance, is surrounded by street urchins playing in filth and muck in the sewer of a river. And these kids look happy and well off, even fat, in comparison to those in the south, in my village, picking lice out of each other's hair, fighting over eggs, and living in clouds of flies.

"I want to be clear: I am not doing this for Shiva, or Allah, or Jesus. I am doing this for those who are suffering. If I just kill myself, it will receive one day of local attention. If that. No, I have to take somebody with me, preferably a rich person, preferably a person whose country can do something, and most preferably, as marketing would most strongly recommend, a pretty blond girl if possible. I am sorry to have to take another's life, but it's the only way that my action, my martyrdom for the suffering, will be remembered. A tragedy must befall a pretty face, for my message to be heard far and wide. This world has taught me that much.

"What else am I going to do? Get married? Have kids? What? So I can watch them die of malaria or starvation? Watch them play in sewage, if I am lucky? If I don't die in childbirth? No. I know how to get people's attention. I have a chance, been offered a chance, been offered the tools, to actually change things. To actually make a statement that will be heard worldwide. I am going to take it."

It wasn't clarified who offered her "the tools." Perhaps on the diary's missing pages she had described this interaction. The reasoning, however, was clear. She had thought it through. She had to do something. And this was something. It was leagues better than nothing.

Mac read it all over again. Appreciating the poetry, letting the words on the page fit back into their grooves in his memory. Like scars finding appreciation for the branding iron. How many times he had wanted to tear up this piece of paper. It still held splattered smears of his spit. And tears. But that was all before the paper started to become thin, yellowing delicate, like sunshine being masked by shadow. He couldn't let it fade, so he had buried it here, in the drawer, under the old lining. Digging it back up intermittently, once a year, to make sure it still existed. To make sure it really happened.

The clipping read now like a tender Dear John letter, the beauty of which he forgot when away from it for too long. He would forget, on purpose, and become angry with her for being in the wrong place at the wrong time.

How can you leave me alone with this? He shook the paper, but it protested stiffly. *Asshole, she was murdered, remember?*

He still preferred to think she had left him. That the reason he was stuck missing her was all his fault. That he must have done something wrong, obviously, something terrible, obviously; why else would he have to suffer this way? It was easier to think this loss was somehow his own doing, somehow under his control, than to come to terms with the fact that fate could be this randomly cruel.

In punishment, he conjured up her smile and let it float around in his mind. It ridiculed him. And it was true, he had occasionally taken its curve for granted—life was full of things to attend to—but now, forever, here it was, as its half precursor, inside the closed coffin, in a steady state of decay, instead of taking flight across her face.

His eyes closed, stinging from the fermented beauty. He put the newspaper clipping on the nightstand. *How could I let myself be robbed? Because it's true, isn't it, that some part of her did belong to me? How could I let it happen? How could I have been so blind?*

I keep losing people. Here. There. Am I cursed?

He felt the pain of the explosion, the horror of dying that way. He was ashamed of it but the thought of her physical pain had always terrified him. It could have been him too. And it was him too. Instead of dying from the pain, he lived with it.

He rolled over. Too tired to maneuver his body properly under the covers, he pulled the far side of the comforter to double over on top of him. Hiding...

Along a back alley in Phnom Penh, a ten-year-old gave his little sister a ride from the rubbish heap in a wheelbarrow filled with recyclables. Their parents, returnees who lost their land, were knee-deep in their rummaging. But they stood straight to watch their children's departure with pride. A boy with no hands, yet another land mine victim, walked past them. His bad karma was decidedly ignored.

Sighing, a young Masterson Peters decided to return to the office. He had additional notes for his survey of eye problems in the squatter slums. His boss, for all of three months now, looked up at his entry.

"So, Mac, do you still want to go to the countryside?" She had a habit of skipping polite greetings whenever possible. "It looks like we'll actually be able to do some outreach services this year. We need someone at the end of December. The province is reportedly 'safe' now." She used four fingers to mock the word. "Mind giving up Christmas?"

She smiled, knowing he would be excited. He had been trying to convince her since he arrived that he was aware of the dangers and was willing to take the risk. His argument always stressed that seeing more of the country would help him do his job better—how could he even try to understand Cambodia if he never got out of the city and saw the rural areas…And now, here, the outreach opportunity was finally burgeoning, almost two months late. She needed someone there; she'd go herself, but she hadn't been home for Christmas in two years, and her ticket was already bought.

She continued in Khmer, testing him, "How are all those language classes going?"

He was eager to impress, and started chatting, while his brain gnawed on disappointing Georgia…

Mac heard movement in the house, someone making a midnight snack. The kitchen, he was sure, was bursting with food ready for the taking. *I am one of the luckiest people alive. And yet, I can't even go through the motions of serving my family? Can't even carve a roast? What right do I have to be depressed?*

It's not about Georgia. She wouldn't stand for that. No, I was lucky to have found her at all.

Under the blanket, he was suffocating in his own sour exhale. He peeked his head out. His vision worked against his will. A window pressed against the side of his bed. The ledge was peeling with paint. Through its glass, some hazy stars taunted his distance, his triviality, his impotence.

Making a myth for a star is not really lying, is it? He hated to think he might be lying to himself, thinking the stars were solid, the light was present, not an eternity old. *But it is still a guiding light, even if at this point it is no more than a story.* He continued, placating himself, feeling entitled, *my memory, my view of the star now, is mine to do with whatever I want.* He realized his lip had swollen into an obnoxious pout.

Oh, come off it, you brat. You're the liar. All you really want to do is stay in bed. You want to bury your head in the sand. You want to face little tragedies, like caramel, matching plates, dirty diapers, your gut, and being dumped by your girlfriend because you don't treat her well enough.

But it was too late. He had already seen. There was proof in the yellowing print cradled by the nightstand. In the sunshine warming Cambodia, reflected to his room by the moon.

At a large urn of collected rain, mid-day light glinted off the water as it streamed from her ladle, through her *krama* scarf, and to the ground. The woman, in an unnecessary frenzy, was cleaning her baby's diarrhea out of the all-purpose cloth. Should she follow the health teacher's advice and give the child mangoes and add more greens, eggs, and fish to the rice porridge, or was her husband's mother right, insisting that it was the meat, fruit, and vegetables that were causing the diarrhea? Should she go behind the matriarch's back and send a request for those shiny packaged salts? It had been three days already and the toddler's skin looked flat; her hands left a lingering impression every time she touched him. And everyone had conflicting advice. She directed all her raging indecision at the red-and-white checkered cloth, scrubbing it clean in a small bucket, rinsing it with the ladle, and then dumping the dirty water out into the pig bin with a furious splash.

For Masterson, the knowledge was easier to bear, if he could acknowledge it was, somehow, however partially, his responsibility. Feeling angry was easier than feeling helpless.

Chapter Thirty-Seven

In the navy air, a knock conquered the room. From bed, Mac looked up at the opening door, to see a rigid figure with a shaking hand. She held a gently sloshing glass and a stoic plate.

"Don't get up; you are obviously exhausted." As she moved forward, her shoulder dropped to the door behind her. "I made you this, this sandwich," her voice quaked.

He was watching her tiny frame with awe. They had never been that close; it was Gramps who played with the grandkids. Elouise was always a little more removed, even when she wasn't so frail. It was as if she was afraid she would become nothing but Grandmother if she acted the part. But here she was, with that stare she used to hang over all the roughhousing with Gramps. The stare of a protective spy, decoding your every movement into its private story.

"Thank you, Gram." Mac, sitting up now, rescued the sandwich and milk from her hands, to set them on the nightstand.

Her eyes settled on the newspaper clipping. Strategically, he nudged the paper over with the glass of milk, trying to hide it. But it was too late. His efforts prompted her to turn her eyes to his face. They shone, reflecting the lamplight back at him, "We never know what's going to happen next, do we?"

Mac blinked rapidly in the reflection. *Does she mean then, or now?*

Veins and knuckles rippled as she moved her hand to her throat. Above her yellow dressing gown, she made contact and rolled dark pearls up and over her collarbone. Back again, fingers becoming entrained in the current.

Clearing his throat, "Your sandwich looks delicious, Gram; thank you."

"Well," shallowly curving out of his room, shuffling with her back to him, "the roast beef is your Mom's cooking and your Dad's carving, so thank them too."

"I will."

Letting the door envelop her once again, she turned against the jamb. "Eat it slowly; it will get you through the night."

So Dad ended up carving after all.

Mac was suddenly aware, now that he saw the sandwich, of having missed a meal, even if his stomach still felt pasted with Brie and onion breading. Underneath it all was the acid burn of gin. And some vague hunger.

On chipped porcelain, a little damp from recent washing, the sandwich was stacked askew. A mattress of pumpernickel was sheeted messily with mayonnaise. Fisted from the top of a head of romaine, dark green comforted torn roast beef. Another layer of bread tucked them all in. In the absence of a knife, Mac pressed the two pillows of

196

pumpernickel together, making the sandwich more manageable, and turning out the lights on the meat.

The spice of the bread hit the roof of his mouth, only to be glossed over by a cool slide of mayo. Another bite and roast beef tumbled forward, trailing fresh lettuce as a playmate. Savory and crisp, a story of competition, chewed up and tossed about in the pumpernickel night. The roast beef was a little dry at first, but quickly becomes slick with mayonnaise, lettuce water, saliva. There was gamey determination in the chew, and a playful rye sting in the bite. It disappeared, folded asleep in the bedroom of his mouth.

It was the first thing that he had tasted in months.

The milk went down as cold and thick as moonlight. He stopped once for a breath between gulps and looked at it, licking his lips. He felt it washing down his throat, cooling his ribs, and bathing his stomach. Its soft light tempered the glare of digestion.

Wiping his mouth with the back of his hand, he swallowed again, unnecessarily. There was a film of flavor in his mouth, milk coating the roof, roast beef residue against the molars. The taste lingered, dotted starry by the spice of pumpernickel and the bitterness of romaine.

He lay back into his pillow. And sleep came like a wet rag over his eyelids. He dreamt he was in a hut, receiving a traditional remedy for eye problems, water dripping through palm leaves onto his lids. Even in the dream, Mac was aware that the treatment was ineffective, but he was hungry for the care and attention. With each drop, sleep absorbed him.

Chapter Thirty-Eight

Putting his hand to his ear, the man leaned dramatically toward the crowd of kids. Girls squatted in the dirt, holding toddlers between their knees; one slapped at a nearby brother, *pay attention to the puppet man*. This time, more kids called out the answer. The man straightened, scratched his head, and looked behind himself at the curtain strung between two trees. Finding nothing, he dipped to look between his legs. All the kids laughed. Their laughter only further bewildered him, and he started grumbling in Khmer. He obviously hadn't understood. They'd have to say it louder.

"What am I supposed to do after I make a smelly?" he asked again, sounding genuinely confused.

"WASH YOUR HANDS!"

The man trembled backward. "Oh. Why didn't you just say so?" He wiped his hands on his shirt.

The kids were slow to react, but one by one they started to murmur, "Nooo."

"What's wrong?" The man mimed, reaching for a mango. They all started screaming. He called on a barefoot girl standing in a sarong and a faded Betty Boop T-shirt. She mimicked, from the original singsong refrain, "Use soap or ash to clean your hands."

Kacham, from the edge of the audience, smiled. This local NGO had done a lot of good here. Their hand-washing push alone had reduced cases of life-threatening diarrhea by thirty percent. And they seemed to be making some progress in the realm of night blindness as well. They had brought half a dozen children to his clinic this year.

Finished for the day, Kacham returned to the shade under a communal hut to pack up the cooler. All outreach health-care programs, including animal and human vaccinations, took place here. Makeshift tables strutted in front of the hut's support beams, which were postered with dirty teaching aids. Circles and squares held pictures of nutrition-rich foods: mango, taro, carrots, cabbage, breast milk, and frogs. Another weathered poster illustrated proper cooking methods. Kacham imagined women squatting on the ground, watching as a village health volunteer made fortified rice porridge on the plastic-sheeted table, kids waiting patiently, but hungrily, for the class to be over. A hammock swung empty in the shade, and a scrawny chicken ran underfoot.

He decided to pay a home visit to the first child brought to his clinic. As he approached the hut, one of five siblings spotted him and elbowed Ry. Down from the shade of the palm-leaf roof, Ry came running to meet the doctor.

During the day, Kacham knew, Ry had always had normal vision. His mother had bragged about his love of reading, and the boy could talk endlessly about games of bottle soccer with the other kids. But

199

since he was two years old, his vision would fail after dusk. Night blindness was common, so his parents didn't worry. *"We like our kids to stay close to home after dark anyway."* But a staff person from the local NGO had explained that night-blindness, if left untreated, could lead to total and permanent blindness. Gaining the parents' trust, he had brought Ry to see Kacham.

Seconds from throwing his arms around Kacham's waist, Ry changed his mind, and ran back to the hut. He scrambled up the ladder, and fished two pieces of paper out from under the grass mat. One had a string of tic-tac-toe games on it. He excitedly showed Kacham which games were his victory. The other paper was homework with all the answers correct. Both would make any child proud. But these made Kacham proud too. Twelve months ago, before the three doses of vitamin A had been given, Ry had been unable to see by the light of the petrol lamp. Dusk meant it was time to sit quietly and avoid accidents, while his siblings finished their homework and played games.

As he showed off, Ry's smile seemed to be in a steady state of spreading across his face. Kacham ruffled his hair, and talked to his mother about her other children and her attempts to plant a vegetable garden. As he praised the seedlings, the shadows ticked forward and the sun sent a glimmer to the other side of the planet.

Chapter Thirty-Nine

Luggage checked. Suddenly free hands felt the need to fill themselves again. Luckily, there were plenty of shops in the terminal provided specifically for that purpose. He realized he had no one in Cambodia for whom to bring back presents. Maybe his maid? His driver? His Cambodian co-workers? His fellow expats, many of them, would have also just been in the States.

He looked passively at gadgets in Brookstone, not even making an effort to comprehend their use, thinking of the medics, his sort-of friends, *maybe if there wasn't such an age difference...*Radath and Kacham had finished their medical training and moved on to private practice, only occasionally still helping with out-reach vaccinations. He hadn't seen them in years. His former boss had returned to the States to give birth, after promoting him. *Why haven't I moved on?*

He remembered the driver who took him to Angkor that one time. In Mac's memory, the man's smile over a Marlboro broadened into

Sree's, the motorcycle driver's, laughing at him. And then broadened even further, into the never-ending spread of lips at Bayon. The last believed in him. *Maybe it is time I go back there,* he thought, passing a metal detector, glad his belt hadn't set it off, for once.

He grabbed a coffee, making it a sickly sweet one, with whipped cream and a clever name, not because he wanted it, but because, in a matter of hours it would be impossible to find. Two stores later, a glossy vitamin boutique displayed sleek synthesized food for those who considered eating real food too messy, not to mention time-consuming. Why eat a salad when you can swallow a pill? Why dirty a pan with eggs when you can eat a chocolate protein bar on the go?

From slanted shelves, shiny packages boasted how their contents had been manufactured (i.e., no dirt ever involved) specifically for him, with his needs in mind. He picked one up. Bright superman colors caped the Superfood, which was ready, and waiting, to rescue him from all the perils of nonspecific foods. Give over those kryptonite bills, the plot commanded, and the super bar would be released. It would circle around his world with such velocity, it would cause the spinning to reverse, rewarding him with the body and health of a man five, no, ten years younger…

Mac put the bar down, and picked up another brand. "Newly improved taste," it read. "Chocolate macadamia nut cookie dough." Rubbing his gut, he reconsidered the Atkins diet as he read the nutrition information. He tried to conjure faith in the mystical power of carb reduction. His nutrition training said no, not healthy, but he had to grant that he felt fuller for longer after eating an omelet than after eating a donut. There was satisfaction in protein, he would admit…

The hungry eyes of an Indian man in a vegetarian restaurant— *there was a friend, a potential friend*—wishing for adequate eggs.

Wishing to be non-veg...*I should really go back there; one afternoon was not enough. I have so much left to see.*

He put down the no-carb brick, and found himself among the bottles.

Perhaps I could bring...It should be oyster-derived of course, slower metabolizing; that article said that shell is synthesized usually at night, when feed is not available. Maybe calcium isn't the problem. It's still worth trying. Maybe there isn't a problem anymore; it was a long time ago. Perhaps they found a cooler spot for the chickens and that was enough to remove the curse.

His thoughts continued to jump around, uncommitted to any one area. *Eggs are a good source of VA; maybe we should look into that? Might be better bioavailability.*

Maybe his butter chicken is available now. Mmmm; would Atkins approve of butter chicken? If I steer clear of the nan?

He might have left, gone back to India. Thailand. Whatever happened to his boy? Maybe he is still there, struggling with tourists and masala dosas.

Might as well go and see.

There was a clock behind the cashier's head. Its lines defined his plane's boarding time. Mac knew, from countless flights, that he had at least twenty minutes; no sense rushing to stand in line with all the people who were anxious about flying. It was the same every time: the slow parade to portion a boarding pass, the large fun steps down the ramp, and then the inching through the cabin as people struggled to lift additional luggage into the overhead compartments.

But in truth, as much as he felt the boredom of repetition settling in, each time he had boarded a plane, it had been a little different.

He arrived at his gate and suddenly felt a guilty for being the last to board. He smiled sheepishly as he handed the waiting attendant his pass. She divided it with impatient skill. But no harm done; the passengers were still backed up, swaying on the ramp, looking futilely ahead…just like always.

But today his reason for boarding an airplane to Cambodia was not to find himself, like maybe it was that first time. Nor to prove himself, like it was soon after. Nor to fulfill a sense of duty. Because we never arrive at these destinations.

No, today, he was returning home to Cambodia, not to relieve guilt, not as an attempt to pay the world back for all his good fortune, nor to find peace and redemption. But only to look and see what he could do…Returning with enough curiosity about the next bite to get him through.

To shield himself from the awkwardness of standing in an enclosed space with a line of strangers, he looked at the plastic around his wrist. Weighted by the oversized bottle of oyster calcium, the bag swung with the heaviness of a clock pendulum. It wasn't much, a simple gift, not a Christmas gift or a birthday gift, just an everyday gift…

www.ingramcontent.com/pod-product-compliance
Lightning Source LLC
Chambersburg PA
CBHW070824180626
46818CB00001B/389